MANGO SUMMERS

SHORT STORIES FROM THE KEY WEST AUTHORS' COÖP

Mango Summers is published by KWAC in association with
Perky Press • P.O. Box 1621 • Key West, FL 33041-1621

ISBN: 0-9668854-2-2

Library of Congress Control Number: 2001119373

Printed in the United States by Morris Publishing
3212 East Highway 30 • Kearney, NE 68847
1-800-650-7888

TABLE OF CONTENTS

THE END OF THE RAINBOW

BOB MAYO

Mack stepped off the Greyhound into the scorching humidity that is Key West in October. He collected his luggage from the underbelly of bus number forty-three forty-one, a Silver Eagle he would remember. It had been a two-day trip. He stepped away and headed outside the small terminal that led to Duval Street and the rest of his life. It was Halloween eve, 1965.

He settled into an upholstered red booth at the J and J Steakhouse and ordered the T-bone with fries and a salad drowned in bright French dressing, watching the main street of his new life out the window while he waited. He began to smile almost immediately, he could smell happiness on its transparent wing, soaring at him. Lucky, that was it, he felt lucky.

Mack dined like the hungry man he was, had something called flan that the waitress mentioned for dessert, smoked himself a Lucky Strike slowly afterwards and left the restaurant grinning.

Two blocks down the street he rented a room at the Southern Cross Hotel with five of his thinning collection of dollars. He'd be needing work soon, lucky or not. Outside the main entrance of the hotel he could see west down Duval to where it ended onto the main ship's channel. It drew him like a wet magnet.

Mack lessened his pace soon after he started the walk, struck by the beauty of lush green trees bursting with brilliant nuclear orange Poinciana blossoms. People on the street carried themselves gracefully in the shades of late afternoon to unhurried destinations. Mack, in slow step with them, headed to touch the salt softness of the Gulf of Mexico. The waterfront area at the end of Duval teemed with shrimp boats, fishing boats and a large shipyard.

The Havana-Madrid cocktail lounge sat on the west side at the end of Duval, where its large sign said the place did not close, ever. Mack noticed Navy boys around the front entrance, on the look, like Navy boys.

He waded into the shallows, his shoes and socks in hand and dug his heels into the sand, trying to anchor his new life with a salty symbolic gesture. He felt good about it, his grin pasted in place. The sun was four fingers from setting due west of him, behind what he would soon learn was called Christmas Tree Island and was sloshing purple and crimson onto low clouds near the horizon that astonished his senses and he said loudly to no one and everyone, "Thanks God," and bent his head in simple reverence.

When he left the water he sat on the curb with his feet on the bricks and looked up the lazy street that led all the way to the Atlantic Ocean. He was shaking the sand from his socks when he noticed the big two-story house diagonally across the intersection. There was a hand-painted "Laborers Needed" sign nailed to the front door of the house.

Mack slid back into his shoes and walked over with excitement. Labor was one of his specialties. The large home had been gently shaded by two huge banyan trees, one on each side, for many years. The trees and the house had grown old together the way trees and houses do, and they blended into one another. Its two stories had been whitewashed long ago, and had been trimmed once with gray paint that had detailed the intricate gingerbread some old shipwright had created while ashore. There was a sturdy widows walk at the gables that offered a queens view of the harbor and out islands.

The contractor Mack found behind the house told him it would be torn down, starting tomorrow at seven. Mack said he'd see him then, stepped back out onto Duval and headed for the Atlantic Ocean. Things were good.

Around the corner from Mack and his new jobsite, up Whitehead Street two and a half blocks, Sgt. Ernesto "Ernie" Cruz was kissing his two small boys goodbye on the front porch of his small frame home. He went on shift for the Key West

Police at six every evening, returning 10 to 12 hours later, depending on many things. Ernie led a busy life inside the hot tropic streets he patrolled in the dark.

There was another woman, and such a woman. Her name was Angel, christened Angelina, shortened when her career choice had become evident around seventeen. Ernie had been in love with her since; she knew it, and had charged him for sex, like the others, every time. She lived back of the Havana-Madrid and rarely left the property. Angel weight three hundred pounds, every corpuscle filled to the brim with uncanny sexuality and grace. She had been perfectly named. She was very popular.

Ernie stopped by her rooms on his way to work, the smell of his children's wet kisses still clinging to his sloping mustache. She poured him a cafe con leche and they sat together on the small wooden porch facing the last of sunset together, quietly like an old married couple, until the fire extinguished into the ocean and the strong coffee was gone. He rose, leaned over and kissed the top of her massive head and left for his nefarious duties. It was a normal start to both their evenings.

Mack strolled his good luck back up Duval to the Southern Cross, stopped at a place called Delmonico's for a cold beer on the walk, felt a little strange there, and left after one.

He showered down the hall in the communal bath, felt he could see the Greyhound going down the drain, the bus seemed a long time ago, back before he had a home, and he was happy to wash it away. After he shaved and hit himself with Old Spice he changed into clean jeans and a fresh T-shirt and headed back out into his night. He could smell a little romance riding the wind with his luck. It'd been a while. He'd been in love some, and liked the danger.

His new permanent smile widened like his strides toward the south and the ocean. The streets were quiet and dimly lit. Smells of fish frying wafted over from side streets and reminded him of food again, the pungency tantalizing. Spanish music from small radios blared softly with the sounds of Havana, ninety miles straight down Duval, close. The missile crisis still on the town's breath. The bolito numbers came in the afternoon from Cuba on the same radios and caused delight and strife, like everywhere.

At the ocean he sat inside Logan's Bar and toasted the Atlantic, then took a beer to the dark beach outside, shoes in hand again and waded into the water. He looked up at the night sky for the first time and lost himself in its diamonds, alone and happy to be alive in such beauty.

He was leaning against a coconut palm tying his shoelaces when the police cruiser pulled smoothly into the last parking spot at Logan's, close to him. The officer jumped from the cruiser quickly and entered the side door of a white Ford van. The van left the parking lot and turned right on South Street. Mack thought it a little odd, finished tying his shoes and had another beer. Logan's was having a slow night. Mack remembered hunger and love, was starting to get a buzz, and headed back downtown.

She had seen him from the window where she was washing her enormous red brassiere in cold water at her kitchen sink. Saw his tall stride and his head up smile, watched him wade and felt his happiness when she saw him pray and shake the sand from his socks. She sighed heavily when he disappeared behind the Tolbert house, and wiped her brow. "That one," she said in her throaty Spanish to herself, "makes me wet and weak in my knee, aye, ya, ya."

So at eleven when he walked through the swinging doors of the Havana-Madrid cocktail lounge she saw him right away from the back booth, her booth. She got wet and weak of knee, as expected. He walked right at her heaving chest and sat down on the last barstool, his broad back to Angel, a good thing. She fanned her beautiful flushed face furiously, long eyelashes blinking like the Sand Key light. Love was in the air all right, with heavy, Spanish wings.

Truthfully, she'd be hard to miss under any circumstance. There was her size of course, but that was only a fraction of the attraction. Rooms changed when she entered, and she was clearly in control of the folks in them. Tonight she wore the red satin low-cut outfit from a mail order place in L.A. that catered to her special needs. Mack noticed the great bosoms and the beautiful face above them in that order, flushed and walked to the closest barstool, sat down and immediately felt his neck reddening from what could only be a gaze from her, ordered another beer, his voice failing him, two octaves higher in the forgiving dark of the barroom. He drank deeply from the bottle and cleared his throat conspicuously. He smelled her perfume, jasmine, all over him, gave up and swiveled the barstool to face her.

"I'm Mack," he managed to use his normal octave.

"Sure you are."

Her accent melted him and he sat down across from her without asking. He couldn't think of a thing to say but managed to look deeply into her dark, dark eyes and lose himself there because she was looking at his soul.

All was lost.

Ernie had ridden to Stock Island with the two soon to be burglars in the Ford van. They stopped at a house behind the dog track and parked the van under a small carport. They loaded it with air hoses, acetylene torches, the largest boring drills Ernie had ever seen, rope, extension cords, miner's hats with mounted flashlights, two long extension ladders, four small air tanks and two tool chests. Everything was packed methodically into two large duffel bags and checked off a list then were loaded inside the van. The last item on the list was food, which they would do late Halloween afternoon, tomorrow. There was little chitchat.

The two men drove Ernie back to the patrol car at Logans and disappeared back up South Street. Ernie opened the trunk of the patrol car and extracted a brown paper bag and its rum bottle from under the spare. He opened the cap and pulled heavily from the contents. It was a nervous evening.

Mack opened his eyes at five, the salt of their lovemaking in his nostrils. Outside, the slow morning would unfold where he would be working across the intersection from Angel's fantastic breasts, where his head lay. He'd be keeping an eye on the backside of the Havana-Madrid, that much was certain. She stirred under him and Mack closed his eyes and nuzzled against the greatest nipples in the world for a few minutes more then slipped silently off the bed, dressed and left her sleeping. No money had changed hands. He took the look on her sweet face to be a satisfied smile.

He checked out of the Southern Cross and carried his belongings down the street to Shorty's Diner for breakfast before work. The meal was as agreeable as the air outside, full of optimism and hot tropical possibility. He hurried the two blocks to work, arriving early to talk the contractor into letting him care take the house for the weekend, his hotel days now hopefully at some sort of end. He threw himself into the job with two slow movers sporting obvious hangovers but by noon the two outbuildings were dismantled and loaded onto stake bodied trucks and hauled away. His two co-workers did not return after lunch and he worked alone inside the main house, carefully extracting the heart pine wallboards and stacking them for re-use.

Mack worked steadily until six. The contractor gave him 50 bucks, said he hoped to see him again on Monday and left him to his holiday home. The house was void of furniture but the water had been left connected so he took a cold refreshing shower and changed into clean clothing, ravenous and thirsty for the night ahead.

He made a makeshift pallet from some fairly clean tarps up on the widows walk overlooking the town and harbor and noticed in detail for the first time, the monolithic brick bank across the street to the left of and also across from the Havana-Madrid. If things didn't work out with Angel he figured to fall asleep watching the stars right there.

Ernie had come home at noon too drunk to eat. He passed out on the sofa in the front room with cartoons blaring at his pajama-clad children, mesmerized wide-eyed mouth-open putty at the hands of the television networks in New York, but he took no notice and slept the entire afternoon. His wife Yolanda, also in pajamas, spent most of the day complaining about him to her mother in Miami by phone.

He awoke at 5:30 puny and hungry. He ate black beans with some yellow rice from the pots on the stove with Cuban bread. Then he shaved and changed into a fresh uniform and left the house without a word. He parked the cruiser by the bank across from the Havana-Madrid, walked around the right side to Angel's quarters and stepped in unannounced.

Mack had watched his every move when the cruiser pulled up next to the bank from his high hidden perch across the street. He also recognized the officer as the same one from the parking lot at Logan's last night. Curious. What was going on over at his new love's place? He decided against barging over and interrupting and held his ground, watching the streets below come alive with early revelers as they roamed lower Duval, thick with Navy and teenagers, car horns blaring, skeleton outfits and monkey masks ducking in and out of shadows.

He liked his perch with its incredible panorama of the island and wondered sadly why it was being demolished. The crowd thickened after sunset and Mack noticed for the first time the white Ford van had pulled up behind the police cruiser across the street. Shortly the officer came away from Angel's where her soft lighting had come to life for the evening, nodded slightly at the van and walked across the street, under Mack, and headed up Duval, leaving the cruiser fronting the van.

The police sergeant walked casually up Duval one block to Greene Street and turned left there, across from Sloppy Joe's Bar. He crossed the street, glided past the empty city hall building and walked into the dark backyard of the two story empty house on the corner. The home had been for sale for two years but had no takers at $22,000.

Ernie looked closely about, felt secure with what he saw, and entered the back porch by the screen door. The back door to the house was not locked. He took the gas can that had been left there and spread its contents around the floor of the bottom story, moving quickly in the darkness. He retraced his movements to the back door inside the fumes that stung his nose, spilling some of the gas on his black patrol shoes, soaking his socks. He slid the can across the linoleum kitchen floor, stepped outside the back door carefully and threw a struck match on the floor. He slipped in darkness out to Greene Street and was turning the corner onto Duval before the flames engulfed the bottom floor and began their climb toward the hot pine walls upstairs. Key West's two great fears are fire and water. It was going to be a big fire.

Mack had come downstairs and sat on the steps of the dark front porch when Ernie came scurrying back past him, ran across the street and disappeared behind the bar. Mack stayed in the shadows watching for the next development when the first siren began to wail. Seconds later the acrid smell of fire came on the breeze from the south and permeated the area. He looked in the siren's direction and saw people running to the left up around the neon Sloppy Joe's sign.

He started toward them, then changed his mind and went back inside the house and up to the top and his stage to the island to keep multiple tabs, overcome by a strange sense of wonder. The bar across the street emptied and the entire section of town was suddenly deserted. Fires are a big draw. Mack looked to the south and saw the huge glow then began to literally feel the heat. The winds had picked up and embers were quickly in the air. Multiple sirens wailed in the Halloween night. The Key West policeman came running from the back of the Havana-Madrid and jumped into his cruiser. He snapped on the siren and emergency lights and sped up the street to check on the fire. The white van had not moved.

The burglars entered the National Bank of Key West via the newly built outdoor luncheon and break deck off the second floor. They pulled the extension ladders up after the bags of gear had been hoisted and cut the alarm free glass in the new doors to gain entry into the bank proper. No one was on the street below and the break-in went undetected.

They made their measurements quickly and put on surgical masks and ski goggles. In forty minutes they busted though the thick concrete that separate the two floors and more importantly, the ceiling of the safety deposit box room directly below them. No alarms sounded.

They turned off the big drills and their noise and widened the opening with four mighty blows from the big sledgehammer. They tied off a big rope and slid down into the room of treasure. Trick or treat.

Mack could no longer resist the huge fire's attraction. He joined most of the rest of Key West at the scene. All three of Key West's pumpers were now pouring water not only on the house, but those around and nearby. A fire this size could wipe out the downtown completely and everyone knew it. The hot yellow tongues of flame lapped like whips at the night and all else they could touch. Mack looked around at the revelers, eerie in costume against the fires wicked pitches, now quiet as a funeral. Halloween had been burned out and replaced by real fears. Mack felt a part of them, thought once again of Angel and turned away from the fire and walked toward her. As he was passing the house he remembered leaving the fifty in his workpants. Once upstairs he went out to the widow's walk to light a cigarette and check the fire again.

The dust was so heavy inside the vault they decided to climb back up to the second floor and let things settle. Once there they broke out two Cuban sandwiches. The larger one crawled out to the hallway and burgled two cokes from the machine by the double glass doors they had gained entrance through. He forgot that the light on his miner's hat shone brightly at everything he faced while getting the soft drinks. That's when Mack saw the dancing lights inside the bank from his eye level perch across the street.

Mack never considered calling the law, since from what he could figure, they were already on the case. What he did do was duck down and continue watching until the dancing light moved elsewhere in the bank. He was pretty excited. Hellacious, probably arsenous fire up the street, bank heist here, what a town. He was home at last.

Then there was Angel across the street and that could use some rethinking too, unless he missed his bet. Did luck come in a disguise this thick or this transparent? He figured to keep a close watch on the bank and the Ford van and that he could do it from the Havana-Madrid cocktail bar, diametrically across the intersection.

The bar was empty, not even a bartender. Mack laid a dollar on the counter and stretched across it to retrieve a Budweiser. He took a deep breath and walked around to Angel's door. The fire, bank and the rest of Key West could wait. He tapped lightly on Angel's door and called her name.

She let him in quickly. He smelled the gasoline immediately. The shoes and socks were airing in the open window that faced the channel. Mack vaguely wondered about the cop's footwear up at the fire. He took her big wonderful face in his hands and kissed her softly.

She gathered his balls gently with her plump well-manicured hands and led him to the bedroom without a word or choice.

"Do you know about the bank job going on across the street?" Mack whispered.

She released his balls, "I'm pretty sure I know about the fire. Are we in love?"

She grabbed them again, not so softly.

He winced. She held on.

"More than I ever thought possible." Mack did know some things about love, and he was in a real position to tell the truth.

"Are we going to grow old together and have fat beautiful babies?" She was looking deep at his soul again.

He was lost. They both knew it. Things would never be the same again. It was for Mack a time of truth like no other. He said, "You're my pot of gold at the end of the rainbow."

She said, "Then I guess I know something about that burglary across the street."

The Devil with the Wheeled Garment Bag

THERESA FOLEY

Damien, the houseguest, entered Mia's life through two parted, sliding doors that led to the tarmac at the Key West International Airport. Her visitor floated smoothly through the smudged glass like a mirage towing a wheeled garment bag. They embraced, cautiously, tentatively after eight long years of nothing more than electronic connection. An awkward, short wait at the luggage carousel produced four massive bags, enough gear for a move around the world.

Perhaps there should be a statutory time limit on houseguests but there isn't, and Mia had been feeling generous when he suggested a month. Thirty-five days. "We need plenty of time to catch up on all those years," he'd said.

Damien Allen was 50 and in fine form, fair, with pale and freckled skin, a trim waistline, chin dented by a charming, perfectly centered dimple. He wore his hair in the same wiry, blow-dried helmet as before, a style leftover the days when as an aspiring actor, he'd landed a series of small movie roles. He was attractive. And single. They had certain things in common but being single at the same moment had not been one of them until now.

She drove him home and settled him into the guest room that she had carefully prepared with clean sheets, a handmade quilt, and a small workspace. Then they headed into town for a long walk and dinner at Caribe Soul, where he told her he wasn't interested in food. Too many time zones that day.

Back at her conch cottage after dark, she suggested a swim, saying, "The pool's heated."

Immediately, she began to worry. Swimsuits or no? She always swam naked when she was alone in her private garden with its six-foot fence. But moving from a trans-continental flirtation made up of computer bits and bytes straight into naked in the swimming pool was a little too jarring for her, even if they'd been friends forever.

It had never been clear what the computer flirtation was about anyway, since it crossed borders at random: "I'm naked under the sheets as I write with the windows open" he'd tell her. Once he pretended he was there and the words "running my finger up your thigh until I reached the seam" formed on her screen as if some seductive entity was controlling her keyboard.

She played until the game left her with tears running down her cheeks. Her heart was still broken, and electronic sex chat wasn't going to fix it. The words on the screen asked over and over about her heart, and advised her to "Just love yourself and everything will be all right." On rare occasion, Damien would answer questions about his own past love affair in a Reader's Digest condensed version. He'd had "a long, hard drought" of a year with no sex, the characters on the screen told her.

Why an eligible bachelor like Damien would go without sex for a year mystified her. Now he was coming to stay with her. There'd never been any chemistry between them before, but they were older and more mature now. Maybe the ingredients would have improved with age. After he said he would come to Key West, she asked him about his intentions. "Have you thought of us sleeping together?"

Across the computer screen came: "We'll agree right up front not to. That way, if something happens, it's because it just does, not because we've planned it." Mia appreciated his logic. Spontaneity was good, but so was clarity of intention. And so considering the question of swimsuit or birthday suit on the first night in the pool, she opted for clarity of intention. A few minutes later, she was soaking in the heated water in a favored old one-piece, ten thousand stars twinkling between the palm fronds and bamboo branches overhead.

Damien came out of the house and she was relieved to see a tiny Speedo on him. He carried a miniature stereo system, something that apparently had been stashed away in the bags, along with his collection of music. He set it up by the pool and went back into the house. This time he came out carrying beer and wine, which he set on the edge of the pool and hopped in. He floated around for a minute then came to her.

"How's your back?" he said, pulling her close and turning her away from him. He began to rub her back in the water. This felt nice, very lovely. She sipped a bit of the wine. Five weeks of nocturnal wine drinking in the pool, and she'd be in big trouble. Besides trying to establish some ground rules on the sleeping arrangements, she'd asked him, "What about drinking? I'm afraid I might start drinking too much."

She had been remembering the 20-year-long friendship and how it much of it had revolved around long boozy dinners, endless bottles of wine and large bowls of pasta.

"Not a problem. I hardly drink at all. I'll be too busy working," he shot back.

Now she was waterlogged and sleepy, and she decided to call it a night. "I'll see you in the morning," she said.

Next day she was up at dawn, padding down the hallway in bare feet, past Damien's open bedroom door. She reached for the doorknob, to shut it, so as not to wake him up with her morning tea kettle and cat-feeding sounds.

"You're up," came a voice from the dark bed.

"Mmm. Go back to sleep."

"Come in for a minute. Let's have a little talk."

She hesitated. She wanted her tea and to check the computer and read the Times on line. He called out again. Trained since childhood to be good and do her best to please others, she sat down on the end of the bed.

"Come here." He patted the sheet. "For a cuddle."

She edged closer, suspicious. Why was he being so physical, so affectionate, if he meant what he'd said about no sex, no sleeping together?

"Let's talk about things," he said, holding his arms out. "Come on."

Her resolve softened. It seemed harmless enough. She lay down next to him. Before she knew it, he was asking deeply personal questions about her heart. But she was inside her own head, thinking about the long year it had been since she'd allowed anyone to touch her. She felt the tears coming, didn't try too hard to stop them, and Damien patted her encouragingly.

"It's okay."

She asked him a question. "What about your heart? You've been a long time without someone."

"Ha, ha. I've worked through all that."

"And you're ready to start again? With someone new?"

"The River. I follow the River."

"What does that mean?"

"The flow of the River is my guide. It's got the answer."

She thought about the night before in the pool. The alcohol, the way he seemed to be coming on to her in a gentle, seductive way. "You know, we agreed we wouldn't sleep together. How are you feeling about all that now?"

He laughed. "Hey, a guy my age is happy to find out he can even get it up anymore."

"That doesn't answer the question."

She felt him slide his hand down to her buttock and give it a squeeze. The touch was a shock, as sharp as if he'd stuck a pin into her. She wanted to fly out of the bed, but she was frozen, prone on the bed, glued to his side.

"I would never do that to you," he said. "To start something when I'm about to leave. I really prefer an intimate friendship. Yes, that's what life is about, intimate friendship."

She extricated herself from his arms and got off the bed.

Part of the allure of having a houseguest is the opportunity for a host to fine tune his or her entire life to please the visitor. She liked organic vegetables, black tea, tofu and yogurt. He liked canned tuna, beer and garlic. She was moody and loved solitude; he was gregarious and unceasingly cheerful. She liked broccoli; he thought it had been engineered as a germ trap. "The pesticides get trapped in the crevices," he told her when she tried to serve it.

"This is organic," she said, defending her broccoli.

"Fabulous, marvelous," he smiled. "I never, never, never eat broccoli."

Next Mia took him on a bicycle ride to see the world famous sunset. After two blocks, Damien began to curse the battered second-hand bike she kept on hand for guests. He skidded to a halt and fell over, telling the bike and its brakes to be damned. "Almost lost the family jewels," he grimaced.

So she spent $40 fixing the brakes and getting a proper light the next day, bringing the bike home and calling him outside to check the improvements. Damien grinned at the bike with a "fabulous, marvelous," and then refused to touch it again.

A trip out to see the reef? "Fabulous, marvelous," Damien said, nodding, but when she tried to schedule it, he told her, "I've seen the reef before. I'm here to get some serious work done."

Instead of enjoying the island, they spent their days on their respective computers. She'd arranged the guest room with a cozy work corner, but Damien moved all his gear to the dining room table, telling her that her set up was "bad for my back." Out of the suitcase came a 50-foot-cord and miniature telephone with a headset that looked like air traffic controller gear. He parked it all 18-inches from Mia's desk, so close that she could smell his hair tonic and the garlic on his breath.

On day five, one of Mia's many friends, Cara, dropped by after work. Damien was in the kitchen, chopping garlic and looking for something to cook with it.

"Damien, meet Cara," Mia said.

"Fabulous, marvelous," he said, drying his hands on a towel. "Like a drink?"

"You know, I think I will," Cara said. Her white nurse's uniform set off her blue eyes and long, wavy blond hair, which tumbled halfway down her back. "I've had a long day."

Damien opened two beers. "Have you eaten?"

Cara resisted; Damien insisted; Mia watched the contest from the sidelines. It didn't take long for Cara to cave in to the dinner invitation.

Damien sliced up a pile of garlic with special knives in a kangaroo skin cover extricated from the suitcases as he got acquainted with Cara over the beer. Mia stayed in the corner, washing spinach and wondering if Cara would catch hell from her live-in boyfriend when she didn't come home for dinner.

Damien was telling Cara a long story about how he learned to cook by barging into kitchens of his favorite restaurants and asking the chef and his staff 4,000 questions about what they were up to. When Mia abandoned her spinach and carrots for four seconds to look for a steamer, Damien swooped in and scraped them into one of his pans. He stuck his head in the refrigerator and began pulling out every leftover he could find, and dumping everything on top of the spinach and carrots. Mia watched as a container of hummus, a bowl of tabouli, chile pepper sauce, one chopped up head of garlic, some wine, and last week's pasta and rice remnants were dumped into the pan. She finally had to turn her head. Damien stirred the mystery stew, chugged down his beer and focused hard on Cara.

Then he gestured toward the sink to indicate that Mia might want to start washing as he launched a monologue on Miami politics. His hands chopped another head of elephant garlic into small pieces. He gave Cara a wink. "Like garlic?"

"Love the stuff," Cara beamed back.

"It's fabulous in a salad," he replied.

Mia looked up from washing the dishes. "Raw? Please don't. I can't eat it raw."

Damien scraped the small mountain of glistening white garlic slivers onto the lettuce. "You'll love it. It's good for you. Fabulous." He opened another beer for Cara.

When the goulash was ready, they adjourned to the table on the back deck overlooking the pool. Mia lit candles and Damien brought out a bottle of red wine. As they ate, he fired off probing, personal questions at Cara. The questions were all very familiar to Mia.

One. "Are you in love?"

Two. "How do you know you are in love?"

Three. "Do you really, truly love yourself?"

Somehow, the vague implication hung in the air that you were being tested about love and while you might be able to give an interesting answer, it undoubtedly would not be the correct one. What annoyed Mia most was that he expected you to confess your deepest thoughts, but if you asked him the same question, Damien murmured in an all-knowing fashion, "I go where the River takes me. Trust the River."

Like he had a River, and she didn't. At first she thought this River business was the sign of a deep spiritual well but in the end, his regurgitation of the River grated on her nerves like an old record with a scratch that skipped until you wanted to smash it.

But Cara, glamorous, healing Cara, was a much more accomplished verbal sparring partner than Mia would ever be. By the middle of the meal, Cara was bouncing the probes back at him as skillfully as a tennis champ at Wimbledon.

"Let me ask you something," Cara said, blue eyes shimmering in the candlelight. "Do you think it's possible to be incredibly physically attracted to someone, to be in love with them, and not have sex with them?"

For once, Damien did not fall back on the River. Instead, he replied, "Of course. I have four women I can think of right now who would have the most passionate sex imaginable with me, at the drop of a hat, if I'd let it happen. But we're just friends. Of course, they are all married to my best friends, and I'm an honorable guy, so we never act on it. Each of them is as intimate as any lover could be, and each time we meet it's totally charged with sexuality. We would go to bed in a minute, if only things were different."

Cara nodded her head as if she understood. "So these women are all married."

"Well, not all," he said. "Two of them are married, one is separated and another is divorced."

She nodded. Then he added, "But I would never act on those desires. I respect the men far too much."

More nodding, more wine, then it was time for a swim. Cara led the way, confidently leaving her clothes in a poolside pile as smoothly as a lizard slipping out of her skin and plunging in. Mia shyly went into the house, took her clothes off and put on a robe, then came out to slip into the dark water. Damien meanwhile also had stripped down and was strutting around naked, moving the pool cover. All three were in the water together for a while, but the temperature was well over 100 degrees, and soon Cara was lounging naked on the rocks at the pool's edge to cool down. She looked like a mermaid on those rocks, Mia thought, with her back arched to highlight the swell of those large breasts and her legs crossed demurely, hiding nothing.

The next day, Mia went to the airport to leave on a ten-day trip. In the air over Miami, she thought about the dinner talk. Damien seemed to prefer some imaginary unattainable love affair that could never be consummated but would provide an infinite stream of flirtatious come-on. Much safer to fall in love with unavailable women. That high intellectual plateau was a safe height from which to observe those who struggled with matters of the heart.

A few days later, Mia called him from a hotel lobby in Palm Springs. He asked how she was holding up.

"I miss my cats."

His voice came from the tiny earpiece wired to her cell phone: "Get naked and Have a Martini!"

"Excuse me?"

He repeated his advice to get naked and drunk.

She shook her head. "That maybe your idea of good time but I'd rather go hiking, read a book or go to the spa."

He told her he'd spent Valentine's Day evening with Cara and Judy, another friend. Mia hung up. Did he urge her to get drunk and naked because he was a testosterone-saturated male without any common sense, or was he joking? If he were here, would he take all his clothes off and get totally drunk? And then what? Try to get laid? Not that such a risk seemed likely for Damien with his fear of germs and resistance to available women.

When she flew home a few days later, Damien met her at the airport. She was determined to get the friendship back on track. At home, he made dinner for her, to welcome her back.

After they finished the salad with garlic, with beer as the side dish, Mia went to her computer. Damien settled in at his laptop, putting on the air traffic headset to make some calls. Mia heard him dial, greet someone, and then begin to coo into the phone like a pigeon. Was he talking to Cara? The mutterings sounded like two lovers wishing each other goodnight across the continent, instead of two people who were only four blocks apart.

The next day, Mia ran into Cara's best friend, Judy — Judy of the Valentine's Day party that Mia'd missed out on — at the Java Lounge.

"Thanks for hanging out with Damien while I was gone," Mia said.

"I love him," Judy said. "I love him. We both do. Cara and I are going to keep him. We just can't decide which one of us gets him."

"You can't?" Considering that one of them was married and the other had a live-in boyfriend, this struck Mia as peculiar. But maybe Damien would make a nice pet.

That night they went to a cocktail party, and who did they run into but Judy and Cara. After the daiquiris and martinis and chardonnay had done their tricks, Mia found Judy at the bar and suggested dinner. "Shall we grab those two?" Mia said, steering Judy over to where Damian and Cara were huddled beneath a tall Traveler's Palm at the back of the garden. "Dinner? Antonia's anyone?"

"Oh, I don't think so," Cara said, clutching Damien's elbow and pulling Judy to her. "We want to keep Damien all to ourselves. You just go along, honey."

Mia lurched away, feeling like she'd just been slapped. She scanned the room for other familiar faces until she found Anna and Fred. Her friends took her to an Italian restaurant and patiently nodded as they swapped houseguest anecdotes, the nightmares that are stock in trade for Key West residents.

"Maybe I don't get it. Maybe I'm a bad hostess and need to cultivate southern manners and patience," Mia said. Cara and Damien were probably perfect hosts, spinning their spells over everyone they encountered.

At midnight, she was home in bed, sound asleep, a cat purring next to her when she heard footsteps in the hallway, then the door to her room flew open.

"How are you?" It was Damien.

"I don't know. I'm sleeping."

"Something wrong?"

Mia groaned. "Yes."

"You're kidding. Better tell me."

"I just didn't appreciate being excluded from dinner."

"Excluded?"

"Yes. I didn't expect to be put off by people who I thought were my friends."

"Well, you didn't miss much. The food was no good. Kitchen wasn't clean. Never going back there again."

Finally he closed the door and left her alone. The next night, Damien had a dinner invitation to eat at the home of more new friends. She declined his request that she come along and heard him on the phone with Cara. At six p.m., he shaved and showered, splashed on cologne, grabbed a bottle of red wine from the pantry and ran out the door. Around 1, he was bumping around in the hall again but this time he didn't barge into the bedroom for a late night chat.

The next morning, Damien stayed in his room later than usual. He came out around 10, eyes puffy, skin a greenish tone. His hair had lost the glued-down helmet shape and stuck out like a bad perm.

He emitted a grunt instead of his usual chipper greeting, as he passed her at the computer on his way into the bathroom. Due to the tight quarters of the little house, she had become by now as familiar with the sounds and odors of Damien's morning routine as a life-long spouse. He finally came out, sat down at his own computer, and fell silent. She thought he might be sleeping until she heard him say, "No more wine for me."

That night they went to visit Anna and Fred. Damien told stories about all his movie roles and the countries he'd visited. Anna and Fred hung on every word, but Mia just yawned. As she studied Damien while he worked her friends like a crowd, she noticed how he clipped the others off mid-sentence and then rattled words out in a solid block without a sliver of a crack for another voice to slip in.

When Anna brought out a bottle of red wine, Damien's eyes lit up. So much for the morning's wise resolutions.By the time they got home, they were at the edge of the crevasse. They made their way through the little house to the kitchen, talking about writing and film.

"A few months ago," she said, "my friend Peter in New York suggested that I write a script about a meteor striking the Earth, an end of the world kind of thing, that would be truthful about what people might really do if they knew the world would end in three days. Like make amends with their estranged lovers or family, or go to Paris for a last wonderful meal, or swim with the dolphins."

Damien gave her a look as though she were telling an old joke for which he'd heard the punch line a million times and said, "I know exactly what EVERYONE would do. Eat chocolate, drink whiskey and get laid."

She shook her head. In that order? Everyone?

"Maybe that's what you would do, Damien, but there are plenty of people who would want to something besides eating sugar, getting drunk and having sex with anyone they can lay their hands on. You don't actually believe what you've just said."

"Of course, I do. Drink whiskey, get laid," was his response. "What else is there? Come on."

"No. I won't come on. It's all a big joke to you, isn't it? Don't you think there's anything more powerful that you could do with your life than drinking and talking crudely about sex? I don't know if it's a cultural thing or a gender thing, but the way you make these remarks about women and sexuality is offensive. Is this the way you've been taught to talk about women?"

"Lighten up. It doesn't mean anything. I respect women," he said, defiantly.

"I'm sure you think you do, but I've got to tell you. This thing you do where you flirt outrageously with every woman around is getting real old."

"Flirting? Flirting is healthy. It's good for you. It's fun."

"You've been flirting with me for 15 years and I'm over it. It's not good for me. I've had it with the constant stream of sexual innuendos."

"Hey, I was only teasing."

"That's exactly what I mean. I don't like to be teased."

"What's so bad about teasing?" he asked innocently.

"You don't know?"

"No."

"What do you think teasing is?"

He thought for a minute then said, "Holding out what someone wants, then taking it back."

"Okay. You aren't going to like hearing this. You would never get away with most of the things you say to women if you weren't good looking. An ugly man would get slapped, walked away from and hated for the things that come out of your mouth."

"Like what?"

"Like that thing you said to me the other day about dancing. That was so ridiculous. It was awful."

"What did I say?" He looked stunned.

"You said, 'Dancing is having sex with your clothes on.'"

"Well it is. Dancing is having sex with your clothes on."

"Dancing is not having sex with your clothes on. Maybe once in a while, it might be like that, but if what you say is true, then I've had sex at business parties with bosses that I couldn't stand the sight of, and I must have had sex with a bunch of dirty old men at weddings, or men I would never dream of sleeping with at a bar, just because I wanted to dance. And what about all my friends who are mothers and dance with their children? If what you're saying is right, then they're all having sex with their kids."

"Oh come on," he replied.

"No, I won't come on. You think it's funny. Can't you see that this is a serious subject for women? Sure, we joke about our sexuality but women need to be respected, our sexuality deserves to be treated as something sacred and special, not like it's some dirty joke."

He gave her a look like a saintly child who'd never been punished before and said, "Well, I'm sorry. If that's the way you feel."

The next few days were increasingly awkward. She avoided Damien. He began to spend more and more time with Cara. He did not tell her this but since he had parked his computer and telephone only 18 inches from her work area, she knew far too many details.

Round about day 21, Damien told her his young friend Angel was coming down from Miami. Then he told her the whole thing was off because Angel couldn't find a room on the island for less than $300 a night. "If you want to give up your room and sleep on the couch for two nights," Mia said, "I really don't mind if she stays here."

He accepted the offer and volunteered to go grocery shopping to pick up food for a small dinner party to celebrate Angel's arrival. That night, four women stood around Damien in a semi-circle drinking wine as he mixed flour and eggs and water into dough, then rolled it into pasta and cut it into tiny strips. Three hours later, everyone was getting loopy from wine as they waited for him to hand cut each noodle and lay it on a big rack to dry.

At 11, Mia was lightheaded and starving, and wanted to short circuit the Julia Childs routine. "Anyone want to swim?" she called out. Two minutes later, three naked ladies were cavorting in the hot pool, just beyond the range of Damien's vision at the counter. Even if he stood on tiptoes, he couldn't see a thing. It did the trick. Fifteen minutes later he put dinner on the table and called the wine-numbed women out of the pool to eat.

When the dinner guests left, Mia made up the couch with clean sheets. Angel said goodnight and disappeared into the guest room. At 4 a.m., Mia wandered through the dark living room on her way to the bathroom. In the dark, the couch seemed rather flat. Where was Damien? In the bathroom, the odor of Clorox was everywhere. Damien must have bleached something. Germ patrol.

When Mia got up the next morning, the couch was still empty and the guest room door was closed. Mia shook her head. Damien and Angel were sleeping together. The next night, the same. Damien made the couch up into a bed, then left it untouched.

As soon as Angel headed back to Miami Sunday afternoon, Damien got on the phone and Mia heard the goo-goo noises of verbal affection begin again. She wanted to shout at him, "Get a room! You come to town to play around — you ought to be in a hotel with the rest of the tourists." But she didn't shout anything. Ten days and he'd be gone and her life would go back to placid and boring, just as she liked it. After 20 years of friendship, she wouldn't be the one to throw him out.

When week five finally arrived, a tenuous cease-fire had settled in. One night, he sat around the corner from her desk making baby noises into the phone for twenty minutes before bedtime. "Me too, me too! Oh!! Oh my! Really! Yes, I do too. I do. Yes, yes."

Mia thought she was going to gag. When he finally hung up, she confronted him.

"Would you please take your computer and your telephone and move it all back into the bedroom?"

"You want me to move? Now?"

"Yes."

"Permanently? You're kidding."

"No, I'm not. I'm finding it very distracting." She wasn't going to apologize or point out to him that there was nothing permanent about this arrangement. It had to last two more days.

He relocated but the move only made Mia feel wracked with guilt. How could she treat a houseguest badly? She would make a final effort to do something for Damien. She snared four front row seats to see Kelly McGillis, Key West's own world famous actress, perform Tennessee Williams' Night of the Iguana at the Waterfront Playhouse. Afterwards, dinner at Antonia's. Damian accepted her invitation with a "Fabulous. Marvelous."

Late the afternoon of the show, he ducked out of the house, saying, "Going for a walk."

When he didn't return by showtime, Mia got ready to go without him. She left his ticket on the table near the front door.

At the theater, Damien's front row seat gaped empty as a missing tooth in an otherwise brilliant smile. At intermission Mia searched around for him outside where everyone was smoking but nothing. She got home at midnight, full of fettuccine and wine, and still no sign of Damien.

The next morning, he came out of the guestroom tussle-headed and puffy eyed. After his morning ablutions, he rushed around collecting his knives and telephones and stereo gear, repacking it all into the four large suitcases.

"I looked for you last night. You missed a great show," Mia said to him.

"No, I didn't. I came in, stayed for a half hour. They butchered Williams. It was the worst I've ever seen. I couldn't bear another minute of it, so I left."

"So you just stood in the back?"

"No, no, I had a seat."

She hadn't seen an empty seat anywhere, so he could have been lying but it really didn't matter. Was he so hostile towards women, or just toward her, that he really didn't get it? The visit was over, and they hadn't talked about writing or life or love, and he hadn't even been particularly nice to her, other than to go grocery shopping a few times. What kind of fantasy world had she been dwelling in when she invited him? But he was leaving today; she could afford to be nice for six more hours.

"Look, what time's your flight? I'll drive you to the airport."

"No, no, absolutely not. I don't want to be any trouble at all. I'm calling a cab."

At 2:30, the taxi picked Damien up and he bid her goodbye. "I had a great time. Marvelous. Fabulous." An awkward peck on the cheek.

The next day she went into the guestroom with a big stick of burning sage to smudge away his dark flirtations. Damien had ended his visit properly, leaving a card, with not one but two notes inside, declaring Key West to be full of magic and himself of eternal love and friendship. Mia began to tidy up the room for the next visitor.

BOXMAN

ALLEN MEECE

She was a beautiful boat, a wooden 76 foot shrimp boat. All seventy-sixers are beautiful because they are carved by the sea and they are carved by their work. They have high bows that you can barely see over from the pilothouse. There's a little captain's cabin at the back of the pilothouse with a bunk and a chart table. There's a deckhouse behind the pilothouse that has a galley and bunks for two or three crew members. Usually there are two crew members, a rig-man and a deckhand. Sometimes they'll take an additional person along to make the work go easier but they won't pay him much. He's called the "fourth man" or the "boxman" because he doesn't share in the catch profits. He only gets five dollars for each one-hundred-pound box of shrimp they catch and they'd catch maybe two to eight boxes a night. Five dollars a box for some of the most torturous labor you can do.

I was boxman on the Henny Penny in 1977. There weren't many options for work in Key West. You'd look in the paper for the Help Wanted section and it would be missing. In the summer you could fire a cannon down Duval Street and not hit anybody. Prices were low, the town was quiet and you knew everybody. We had three lawyers in town, now there're at least thirty-three. The Navy had closed the submarine base where a lot of civilians used to work. Key West had again become "the poor man's Riviera," as Hemingway called it in the late nineteen-thirties. But it didn't feel too good when I didn't have beer money, so I tried to get on the boats. When all's said and done, it's the sea that provides.

To get on the boats, I had to hang out where the shrimpers hung out. They had the only disposable income in town and they were able to hang out in nice places that are tourist spots now: Sloppy Joe's, the Half-Shell Raw Bar and Nick's Swinging Doors, which is now Finnegan's Wake, and The Big Fleet which is now PT's Late Night. If they weren't catching much, they had to drink at a cheap little place called The Mascot Bar. It's now an art shop across from the Caroline Street parking lot.

The Mascot was casual. A cement floor, a horseshoe bar, a pool table, a jukebox with lots of shit-kickin' music and a back yard. But the Mascot had standards. You could shout and talk tough but you were kicked-out, eighty-sixed, if you hit anyone. It was for hard-working, hard-playing, friendly people and the few murders that happened were done by misfit outsiders who didn't belong there in the first place. You could never, never smoke reefer inside the bar, you had to go out back for that. The best thing about the Mascot was that shrimpers would come in after a good catch and buy the house a round of drinks.

"Barmaid! Give the house a drink! When I drink, everybody drinks!" they'd shout. Sometimes you'd have three or four upside-down shot glasses in front of you. The place got happy then. Some patrons would file out the side door and into the back yard and it would be quiet for ten minutes like nothing was going on. Then they'd come back in, happier and noisier than before. That's where I chose to seek employment.

There was a little-known "breakfast club" at the Mascot. At seven a.m. when Pervy Flowers, the owner, came in to count last night's receipts and George came in to sweep the place, three or four retired fishermen would arrive to get a cup of coffee with an eye-opener poured in a shot glass beside it.

I found myself there one morning after a sleepless night. Things weren't going too well for me. Just a few dollars and no prospects. Once I had a wife and kids but the corporate lifestyle, with all its lying and cheating, offered no desirable future for me and I left it all behind. For this. Drinking at eight in the morning. My eyes began to burn and I turned my face away from the bar, toward the window, just as the tears came. I breathed deeply to shake the mood and I saw Hippie Dave coming in. He got that nickname because his hair hung below his shoulders like the hippies used to wear.

He came straight to me and said, "We need a boxman, is five dollars enough?"

"Yes."

I was at that point in life that many never have to see, the point where food and a few bucks are enough.

"You've got ten minutes to get your toothbrush and get on board. We're going out for a week or ten days." Then, since he was in a bar, he sat down and ordered a drink.

I was employed! I was leaving the dried-out land and going out to sea on a shrimp boat. I hurried over to the warehouse where I slept on the roof. My "penthouse," I called it. It was where the Hyatt Key West is now. I shinnied up the casuarina beside the wall and got my little bag of stuff and went down to the dock and looked for the highest outriggers in the harbor with the name on the bow that said "Henny Penny."

There she was, looking seaworthy and competent with her Cat engine idling smoothly. She trawled with four nets instead of just two is why she needed the long outriggers. I stepped over the wooden rail and stashed my stuff under the mattress of the empty bunk that was littered with the stuff of the other two guys who shared the space.

"Dave said he wanted me to be boxman on this trip," I said to Matt the rigman and Pete the deckhand who were sitting at the galley table.

"Where's Dave?" Matt asked.

"At the Mascot," I answered.

"Shit," he said. "I'm gonna go get'm." He shut down the engine and stomped off along the dock.

"I'm going too," said Pete, knowing that the bar rescue party always has a few drinks as it tries to convince someone not to get drunk.

I hung around the boat for an hour and went off to join the rescue party. We got underway at nine a.m. the next morning. First we went over to the Singleton Ice Plant, where the Conch Republic bar is today, and loaded crushed ice into the hold. Booty Singleton would put a lien on your boat and advance you the price of ice and fuel and that's how he came to own a fleet of seventy-five shrimp boats. The hazards to shrimpers were mostly on land, in the bars and in the accounting offices.

A shrimp boat can hold ten thousand gallons of diesel fuel. When you start a trip you're already ten thousand bucks in the hole. If you don't catch at least thirty-three boxes you're not going to pay for gas. If that happened too many times, Booty would put his name on your boat and fire you and put somebody else on it that could fish better.

The Henny Penny chugged out of Key West loaded to the waterline with ice and fuel. In the ship channel we lowered the outriggers and she glided past Tank Island, now stuffed with millionaire's houses and called Sunset Key, as gracefully as a long-winged seagull.

On the way out the Northwest Channel, Cap'n Hippie Dave mixed some powder and water in a spoon and sucked it into a syringe and injected it into a vein in his elbow.

"I'm a diabetic," he explained. He went to his cabin and the rigman sat in the pilot's chair, making small adjustments to the autopilot to keep us in the channel.

It was about dusk when we reached the shrimping grounds north of the Marquesas and set the rigs down and the Caterpillar settled into a steady, deep-throated growl at full throttle as she moved the nets and boards across the bottom, eighty feet below, at one and a half knots. As the nets got fuller, she went slower and slower until she almost stopped.

Then it was the winch's turn to groan as we raised the rig. When the nets break the surface, there's always a thrill to see if pink is showing through the net mesh. Well, our first drag didn't show much pink shrimp. We dumped a mountain of stinky trash fish on deck along with one groggy, soggy loggerhead turtle. We put him aside to recuperate. Why he didn't have the brains to outrun a shrimp trawl, we didn't know. The idiot must've swum into the net, trying to poach some of our catch.

Now it's the boxman's turn to groan as he sits on a little stool and bends to the deck and sorts the trash from the shrimp with a little hand rake. I'd get a pile of shrimp next to me before I began heading them, pinching them behind the head with my thumbs and forefingers. The little bastards have needle-sharp horns above their eyes that slide right into your skin and fish juice gets into the hole and stings. Your fingers and thumbs grow long calluses along their pinching edges but when the calluses get wet the sharp horns still go through them. Mad blue crabs can just about pinch off your fingers. Sea cucumbers that we call puke fish invert their stinky intestines and almost make you sick.

The nets are lowered again as Henny Penny starts another drag while you are working on the catch for the next hour. After the catch is sorted comes the pain of trying to stand up. Takes about 45 seconds to stand upright and the spine to unbend. Takes just as long for the legs to get used to being straight again. You send the basket of headed shrimp below, dump it in the bins and ice them down, come back on deck and hose it off just as the nets are hauled so you can immediately do it all over again. It goes on and on through the night. Pink shrimp are night creatures, that's why they've got those big round golden eyes that glow under the back deck work lights.

When the sun comes up the shrimp hide and it's time to rest. The anchor is put out and the engine is shut off and it's quiet with just the slow roll of the boat making metallic squeaks from the rigs. You take a saltwater shower and wash the seafood slime off your hands and rinse your face with fresh water and eat a huge workingman's breakfast. Pete has chummed some yellowtail snapper up to the boat and you two use handlines and catch thirty fish in fifteen minutes before the school wises up and leaves. That's how you make a little "side money." You get to keep whatever you sell the fish for.

You climb on top of the deckhouse to sleep under a shady tarpaulin on the Gulf of Mexico. Clean and fed and tired and resting in a tropical sea breeze, you feel as good as you ever have. You didn't have to go to the office today, you did something real.

You only made fifteen bucks. But, like every fisherman, you're sure tomorrow will be better.

But it's not. It's a little bit worse. Hippie Dave decided to fish his secret hiding place. The shrimp are big there but so are the loggerhead sponges. We got four sponges in the starboard nets and could barely raise them out of the water. The boat heels over and the winch slips with the weight and then two guys have to boost the two hundred pound sponges over the side and it's exhausting. We caught some big shrimp the size of small lobsters but only a box and a half. Still in the red. Although we're working hard, no one's earning their keep.

Matt peed over the rail in the dark and Pete angrily said to him, "Is there no end to your stupidity?" Matt hadn't realized the wind was blowing it back on board and that he was pissing on Pete.

In the morning, thinking it was garbage, Pete threw out some blue crab soup that Matt was cooking on the stove, giving Matt the opportunity for revenge. "Is there no end to your stupidity?" he asked Pete.

It was pretty grim when you had to eat part of your catch. After sorting through a hill of bycatch, the last thing a shrimper wants to eat is seafood.

After some sleep, we start repairing the damage that the big sponges did to the rigs last night. We sew up the rips in the nets and replace some blocks that have deep grooves worn in the wheels by the overstressed trawl wires. A longline boat that had been illegally fishing the Bahamas pulls alongside and Dave goes aboard. They pass up some seafood boxes that are lightweight and show plastic wrappers through the outside layers of ice. Matt stores them in the ice hold.

"They want us to take some fish to the dock so they can stay out and fish some more," was all he said.

That night we caught some really big sponges, almost the size of fifty-gallon drums and they wore out the clutch on the starboard winch and it started smoking and screeching and the shoe rivets cut into the brake drum. Matt stopped it and went forward to get Dave. They came back and looked at the winch and tried it again.

Dave got on the pipe we used to level-wind the incoming cable onto the drum. The cable came in slow and hard and Dave pushed the pipe harder and it slipped from its footing and he tumbled onto the drum and his long hair fed under the wrapping wire and pulled his head down and his body flipped over the back of the winch with a crumpling sound before Matt threw out the clutch and shouted, "Pull him out!"

We cut off his hair with a sheath knife and laid him on the slimy deck and boy was he dead. Gone, just like a statue. There was a dent in his skull two inches deep.

"Cut the rig and get the hell out of here," said Pete, the only one who wasn't in shock. He got out the bolt cutters and cut the trawl wires on both rigs and they slipped through the big blocks at the outrigger ends and swished into the sea. Finito. Trip over.

"Put him in the ice hole," said Matt in a disgusted voice and went up and turned the Henny Penny towards the hill.

We wrapped Dave in plastic garbage bags and duct tape and gently lowered him onto the ice. "Rest in peace," I said, to make it a little more respectful as I iced him down between the big shrimp and thirty gutted yellowtail.

Reaching

J.T. EGGERS

A man defines himself by what he chooses to protect. Should he fight for a woman he may be renowned for his passion. If he excels in battle he will be hailed a hero. And when a man hasn't any fight left in him, when all the lines between heaven and earth have been blurred, when there's no longer any way to tell what there is that's worth fighting for he will be called a boy lost in the darkness. Or, in port-town parlance, a damaged vessel. One with a leak and a list, unable to navigate a linear course.

Dana felt at home with the lost and leaky ships of the world, and that is what led him to drift and to settle, wreck-like, in Key West. There had been the unexceptional semesters at college. His stint in the navy. The short unhappy marriage. The construction jobs. Instead of adding these experiences each to the other, he considered them to have been subtractive episodes, separate and wearing. Time, rum and the relentless South Florida sun mixed to create a potent cocktail, one that allowed him what he felt to be an ease, a peace, a drowsy and—to Dana's way of thinking—well-deserved forgetfulness he hadn't before experienced. And then there was the accident. High noon on a Friday, minutes before lunch, a single misstep at the boatyard. Right there under the very same sun that had begun to restore him, the very same sun that had given him hope, he had slipped off the ladder and landed head first on the pearock.

For a while Dana enjoyed the attentive comments of his acquaintances. "It could have been so much worse," they would say, and he would cock his head piously. "You could have died. You're lucky you can walk." But the game grew old; the bruises healed and the people who had shown so much interest and concern soon returned to the relative comfort of their own petty agonies.

As the soreness left his body he noticed that no matter how it had been seasoned, food remained flavorless. He could no longer taste anything and his sense of smell had been dulled so that even the strongest of scents gave the impression of having come from something far, far away. Dana began to make the rounds of the specialists in Miami, spending money he didn't have only to be told time and time again that his "condition," as they called it, was some kind of freak occurrence, that there was no real treatment, that perhaps one day his senses might return to him as spontaneously as they had left.

There had been something more. In spite of his undeniable physical soundness, there was a certain vitality that had been bled from him out there on the pearock. Even the doctors who hardly knew him, the good ones, could sense it. During the consultation that followed the office visits, completed bloodwork and extensive tests, they would inevitably say to him, "Mr. Gray...Dana...is there anything else? Are you certain you have no other symptoms? Any great stresses in your life, anything like that?" Dana had no answers for these interrogations; he was incapable of assembling a response. He could not put into words how it seemed that the sun had been taken from the sky and plunged deep into a dark barrel of water, nothing left of it but screaming gases and vapor. He could not put into words the removal of desire, the utter absence of expectation. He would simply shrug his shoulders and return home to pore, once again, over the newspapers and telephone directories in search of his next physician.

Lying on the bed, Dana could see the tree through the window adjacent to the dresser. Bright splotches of light bounced off the water contained by a neighbor's small dipping pool and scattered among its leaves in celebration of the impending sunset. The mottled, fluid patterns brought to mind faint recollections of hope, of what he and his life had been like before the fall.

Fat green lobes hung high and heavy on the spindly trunk. Dana propped himself up onto his elbows, trying hard to conjure the taste of ripe papaya. He could not; he had been too long without and the grooves of his memory were worn flat from overuse. The best he could do was to imagine himself devouring the smooth, orange meat. How it would feel cool and soft sliding between his teeth, the juice moving wet across his tongue and into his throat. He found himself to be strangely excited by it and by the simple thought of pulling the fruit from the tree when it was ripe; excited by the thought of how the small shoot had become strong, a tall tree continually reaching for sun and moon and sky; excited by the thought of how small, creamy flowers had fallen open like little mouths, their long tongues swollen and turned to fruit. He imagined the sound of the stem's soft click as it yielded, releasing the fruit into his eager hands. It was an intoxicant.

Elizabeth set her iced tea on the windowsill, where the thick pint glass sweated miserably in the orange heat and disturbed Dana's view. She stood before the mirror and pulled a wide wooden comb through her hair. With a single, practiced motion she flicked it up, winding it around itself and into a tight bun. Stout and freckled, she had never been described as beautiful. She was guileless, and it occurred often to Dana that he had been drawn more to the idea of her than to anything else. What she was was solid. These days his regard for her amounted to the grudging acceptance one might have for a purchase it would be very difficult to return. Once, during the short unhappy marriage, he had bought a couch like that and paid cash for it. A floor model delivered by dark men who spoke no English, it was stained and uncomfortable when it arrived, to stay, in his living room.

Elizabeth stood to dress for work, her red satin robe falling into a liquid pile. Exposed, she made a quick grab for panties, a bra, and the pair of shorts closest to her, white ones tossed limply over the arm of a white wicker chair. The telephone rang.

"Don't get it," said Dana. "It's probably them."

She rolled her eyes and struggled with the topmost button of the white shorts. "Which them? Everybody's them to you these days."

"Fuck," he said, as the ringing continued. "Jesus." He didn't move. "Go ahead. Pick up if you want to."

Elizabeth sighed and let the answering machine take the caller's message. "Have you thought anymore about the things we need to do?"

"Which things?" he asked. He wished she would put on a shirt; her bra was shabby. The polyester lace was worn through on one side to reveal a fat crescent of dark nipple. Dana knew their situation better than anyone. He knew there was no money to buy clothes to hang on the outside of her, let alone what was supposed to decorate underneath. And despite his knowledge he nonetheless considered it, this sight of her, an affront.

"What do you mean, about what." Her annoyance, revealed by the pitch and pace of her words, escalated steadily. "About selling the house, I mean who should list it. About leaving. About doing something. About us."

"No." The house; they had bought it together, fixing it up in fits and starts, living around it rather than in it.

"No, you haven't thought about it, or no you don't want to?"

"No, I haven't had time. "

"Time? You haven't worked since the accident, and that's more than twenty-two months. That's almost two years..." Elizabeth's voice had taken on the insistent carping tone of his mother's. He knew the two of them spoke often and wondered what they said, how much Elizabeth had told her. It was her tendency to tell too much.

"Don't you think I know that? Don't you think I know just how long it's been? Jesus. It's not a game, sitting around here all the time, the phone calls all day, the ringing and ringing and everybody wanting something, everybody grabbing. If I could get rid of that maybe I could get a job or do something. But I can't even think of going out there. How am I supposed to start anything when I can't sleep at night? When I can't taste or hardly smell a damn thing? You think I like this, like being like this?"

She took a deep breath but did not cry. Head level, she fixed her eyes on a spot just above and behind his left shoulder. "You know," she said, "this has been going on too long. I will pick an agent and have this place listed." The words, this time, came out slow and measured, as if she had been practicing them. "All I know is, we can't go on like this forever. I don't want to, and you shouldn't either." She slipped into her t-shirt and sandals and walked to the bedroom door, turning to address the spot a final time. "And I don't know if I can, if I want to, stay here with you like this."

He knew that most of what she had said was true. He also knew that she would stay, that she would return later that night just as she had every night for eight years. Elizabeth was a creature of habit, mouselike in that way, sticking almost without exception to the small and known corridors of her experience and their life together.

Dana retreated to his green plastic chair in the garden where he could quietly sip beer and avoid the pile of unopened mail on the kitchen table. He figured that Steven, the man across the lane, wouldn't want the fruit when it was ready. He probably hadn't noticed it, as his interests leaned more toward opera, large plates of bacon and the stream of couriers and hustlers who came and went at all hours. Proximity, time and the outdoor nature of island life had made Dana acutely aware of his neighbor's most intimate habits in spite of the fact that they hardly spoke to one another.

The tree, as it began, was weedlike, little more than a greenish-brown stick with a few wide, flat leaves. This papaya was not the kind of tropical tree to carry dreamers through long cold winters; it was not lush or graceful or especially smooth. Its trunk was pocked. Its leaves were marked with thick, obvious veins, but it had taken root and flourished fast and tall in the unforgiving soil. When it was small Dana's only view of it was from the kitchen window. As it grew he watched first from the bedroom. Then, from the living room where he could glimpse its right side if he stood at just the right angle and craned his neck. The rains came and before long the sturdy, leaf-crested shaft rose higher than the tops of the fenceposts and was visible from all angles including the sidewalk out front where passers by snubbed it in favor of larger, showier foliage.

The distinctive squeak-hissss of Dana's front gate alerted him to the approach of fresh distraction. Without knocking, a man opened one of the louvered doors. He shut it again. Opened it. Shut it. Open. Shut. Open. Leaving it ajar, he stepped heavily through the house and into the back yard.

"That door sticks a little, man, and y'know you really oughtta plane it down. Just a little bit, and it would be so much better. I mean really. Don't you think?" He breathed in quick and shallow heaves while small beads of sweat pooled and ran down the side of his face. Scratching at a damp clump of hair on his forehead with the lip of a half-pint bottle, he took a long draw before clearing the phlegm from his throat. "Aaahh. Jesus. Hot," he said, and spit into the leaves of a blooming pink bromeliad.

"Hey Alfie." Dana didn't open his eyes, ungrateful for this particular brand of intrusion and the reminder of another task he was supposed to complete but couldn't muster the energy to begin. He wanted to tell Alfie to collect his phlegm, to close the door, to go away and quit bothering him. The words would not come.

"So, what's going on? Wanna go out on the boat?"

The kitchen telephone rang four times before the answering machine picked up. Dana sighed, chiding himself for not having shut off the ringer altogether. His life, it seemed, had become nothing but a series of interruptions.

Alfie, for his part, was neither deterred nor insulted by the cool reception. It was a fact that he hadn't shown much feeling about anything since the war. When his wife had left him, moving and taking their son to California, he had exhibited nothing more than mild surprise. Combat had claimed him. It had broken every last piece of him and left a small monthly check and four fat capital letters, blurred and indelible, on his wrist: USMC.

Alfie gestured to the tree with his bottle. "You know, the rats live in those."

"Bullshit," said Dana. "In what? They can't live in that kind of skinny trunk, hollow or not..."

"No, man, in the fruit. Inside. I'm serious. A few years ago I had one in my backyard and it was loaded. I mean this thing was loaded, biggest ones you ever saw, man, and one day I was watching it, I was waiting for the fruit to be totally ready before I picked it, and I saw a rat come crawling out of one. Chewed his way right through. Agh, it was amazing. So I got out my bb gun and shot the fucker, and then I shot all the big fruits down and when I opened them up, there were rats inside, can you believe it, they had hollowed 'em out and were living in there. Unbelievable. You shoulda seen 'em. Now I won't have one of those anymore. They grow like weeds, though. Wouldn't plant a mamey neither." Talking was an exertion and Alfie was breathing hard again, bobbing his head.

"Hm. Really."

"Yeah, man, unbelievable. It's amazing how little you really need to get by." Alfie shrugged and wiped a forearm across his temple. "Whew. Jesus. So. Think you could loan me eighty? Just 'til Monday, man..."

Again, the words would not come. Dana reached into the front pocket of his shorts and brought out three damp, crumpled bills. "I've got 31 bucks. Take 20. Elizabeth's at work." He hesitated. "Fuck it. Take it all. She'll come home with cash."

"Cool." Alfie reached for the wads and shoved them into his own front pocket. "I've got a few things to sort out now, then I'll come back by. I'll plane that door down. It won't stick. I'll bring my gun for you, if you want, if you wanna shoot 'em down."

"Nah."

"You sure? I mean, you don't want the rats, man."

"Yeah. I'm sure."

"Okay, let me know if you change your mind. I'm gonna go and sort a few things out. Catch ya later. We'll go out and get some shrimp."

"Yeah." He knew Alfie would return in a day or two, relatively sober and contrite, with more or less half the amount of money he had borrowed. Dana locked the front door and returned to his chair, eager only to feel cold beer snaking its way through his system. Shadows spread quickly once the sun went down, but he remained outside, motionless in the night, waiting for Elizabeth to come home and walk upstairs to their bed.

He had always been a poor sleeper. Through the years Dana had learned how to pass the nights without disturbing Elizabeth, and had decided that those few dark hours were the only real quiet ones left anywhere in Old Town. He filled the salvaged cast iron tub with cool water and sat in it in the quiet and dark. The telephone did not ring, and without light the piles of paper and unfinished projects ceased to exist. In the stillness he could feel people sleeping in the houses next door and down the lane. Dana inhaled, concentrating, to savor what he could of the jasmine's cloy and the wet, salt-heavy air.

Though accustomed to the nighttime yowlings and territory wars of neighborhood cats, Dana was disturbed by the intermittent scrapings and quiet shufflings that emanated from the lane. "Too big for a cat," he said aloud. Elizabeth sighed in her sleep and turned as Dana grabbed for a towel and walked to the window, trailing water behind him.

There was someone down there. A man. A tall man, skinny, a shadow, no stranger to dirt or to hunger. He had leaned an old ten-speed up against the neighbor's fence and was precariously balanced on top of the seat. Long, shaking fingers stretched upward from a long, shaking arm.

"Hey you," said Dana loudly. He was surprised by the power he heard in his voice. "Just what the fuck do you think you're doing with my fruit?"

Startled, the man stopped reaching but did not fall and his fingers retracted as though slapped or bitten. He looked up to the dark window in which Dana had so suddenly appeared, shirtless and frowning. The fingers reached up again and pulled hard on the fruit as he spoke. "Nothin' man, nothin'. I ain't stealin' nothin'. I ain't doin nothin'." A papaya dropped into the bike's metal basket with a thud and the hand urgently reached for another. "I ain't stealin'. This ain't your tree." *Thud.* "I ain't hurtin' nobody." *Thud. Thud.*

Dana stood dumbstruck as the stranger tore the tree barren. There was no arguing, the man had been right: the fruit, in fact, did not belong to him. Rage spread through his stomach like whisky, speeding his heart, numbing his fingers, stopping his breath. As he watched the man pedal the ten-speed back out to the street, still shaking and dirty but free and with a basket full of fruit, Dana managed a single quiet sentence. "They're not ripe," he said. The man was gone.

He climbed back into bed and lay there trying to make sense of the lost papayas and the night sky, trying hard to calm himself as his mind raced from one incomplete thought to another. The words had come but they had failed him somehow, the words like "stop" and "fuck" and "no." If he had only known how, he could have tried harder and things might have turned out differently. He could have said the other words, if he had only known them, the ones like "wait" and "please" and "plenty." Yet those words belonged to Dana no more than the papayas had. Words like that were seeded somewhere outside the tight yard of himself, to bloom over other people's fences and fruit into other people's hands.

It was only as the moon slowly arced into view that he became calm enough to smell the jasmine again. He was able to remember clearly how the sun had been shining yellow-white and limitless on the day of the accident; and how close he felt to it so high up on that ladder, the split second before he fell a realization of more than just getting by. Dana slipped a hand beneath the sheet to feel himself, to find the warmth and high curve of Elizabeth's hip, to begin putting order to the chaos.

CONFESSIONS OF A MALE HUSTLER

DAVID A. KAUFELT

I'm a male stripper in a Duval Street Bar. It was once known as Tricks but the new management changed its name to Trucks, having to change just one letter in the neon sign. I'm thirty-two years old but pass most of the time in the dim pink bar light as twenty-eight. I'm of southern Italian descent, as my dad used to say when he was putting on the dog. I have muscles, a couple of tattoos (a blue bird of happiness on each pec, to be specific), a big thick uncut schlong and a six-pack. A never fixed broken nose helps the butch act. I'm a little short, 5' 8" if I stand very tall but really 5' 7". This keeps me from the big time in Miami or New York but still I'm quite a package and Key West suits me. I was born in Philadelphia which did not. Everything goes in Key West, drugs are plentiful if you're into that sort of thing (I am, every once in a while) and the food in the restaurants is mmmm mmmm good. I live in a two roomer on Royal Street in Cuban town. The drag queens next door like to call it Rue Royale. They don't bother me. Nobody bothers me. I got a dog that was billed as a pit bull but she ain't; Joyce is about as tough as a mosquito without the bite. I love the bitch. We sleep together.

There's not much room for any other love life as I'm one very popular dude. The gals are not all of them old and used, like you'd expect. Anyway, those that come cruising into Trucks are usually looking for you can't imagine what. Like I appeal to the kinky — your leather, your body worship, your being tied up and fake raped — but I do draw the line at scat. Also, I always wear protection. My bud Tom died a couple of years ago from AIDS and it was a real lousy death.

Anyway, I will go with guys when I have to (money gets short down here in Key West with all its distractions). When I do do the guy thing, I'm strictly a top which means I don't go down on anyone or any of that shit; the idea makes me want to throw up. But twice in my life I played the woman, biting the pillow every thrust of the way. Seven hundred bucks the first time and one thousand the last time, a couple of weeks ago. I didn't like it but it wasn't as bad you might think. One thousand fuckin' bucks. Count 'em.

Here's my day: Up around two, big breakfast at Camille's and then a couple of hours lifting at Iron Bodys and then a long nap and a thorough shower and then a light dinner consisting of something like a veggie burger and salad. I'm no good in the sack after a big meal. Around ten or eleven I take my place on the meat rack at the snake-like bar at Trucks wearing a white torso t-shirt which goes day-glo under Trucks' neon. Next two hours I joke around with my buds and the queens who hang out there but around midnight the queens know its time for the pros to get serious and the meat rack thins out and the pros shut up and begin to look serious. It's then we start posing, making our biceps hard and/or touching ourselves in suggestive places. For instance, I always have my hands down around my dick, kind of framing it. That's when the ladies and the Johns come in and make their moves.

"You from around here?" (the lady or the John) is the usual starter which finally leads up to "What do you like?" (This from me.) Cash is then discussed. I start at two hundred but can easily be jewed down to one fifty. I've even been known to settle for a c-note depending upon the hour and the demands.

So there's my life in Key West in a nutshell. Sounds sordid to those who don't know but hey, I'm not equipped for anything else and I do look to the future, saving up for the day when I'm an old cocker. I figure I have until forty and then I'll have to go into a different line. Maybe I'll hook up with a broad and run a bar. That's my dream, anyway. *Quien sabe?*

I was pretty happy until the Little Miss May-Be sailed in and screwed me. Sometimes I do a striptease on this party boat, usually for gays but everyone once in a while a straight group hires the May-Be to sail out into the bay, ride around until the sun sets (big whoop) and then comes back in. It's an easy c-note plus tip. The fans tuck bills into my jock as I'm shaking my bootie around to old time rock ("Fame/ I'm going to live forever"). I rarely go the full Monty because even in Key West it gets chilly out there on the water and shrinkage can do terrible things to the size of a guy's dick.

Billy, a former hustler himself, is the owner, the captain and the crew; doesn't take much to run a pontoon party boat but it's even getting past Billy whose leg gives him trouble and whose partner has stopped going out on the boat a couple of years ago.

On this particular night we had a straight-ish group, big time writers no one ever heard of — at least I hadn't — saying goodbye to each other for the summer before they took off for Martha's Vineyard or Europe or some other la-di-dah place. They were moving around the deck, all nervous like, getting tight, the ladies touching me but without the nerve to go all the way, stuffing five dollar bills into my jock. Their guys pretended to be amused but how long can a straight guy get off on looking at my butt bouncing up and down. After twenty *minutos* or so, after the last finsky was pushed into my jock, I faded, got into my shorts and then I mixed with the crowd, swapping stories, being nice and liberal and good humored — hey, like anything goes — until we docked.

This one particular night, after the strip, while I was going around introducing myself, I came up against this sour old codger who refused to shake my hand. I had seen him earlier, not looking at me, talking to a stringy blonde lady, putting away the Scotch like it was designer water, terminal disappointment crinkling his brow, his mouth puckered like he was sucking lemons. Come to think of it, I realize I had seen him before at Trucks, always with a bunch of writers and artists and hangers-on, always three sheets to the wind, avoiding the meat rack at the bar but giving me ugly looks when I happened to see him staring at me.

Here's my personal philosophy: do what you want in bed or out or nowhere, but keep your opinions — and his was as clear as gin — out of my face. I do what I want to do and if I'm fucking your mother or your father or your great aunt Bessie, why that's our biz. We're getting through life as best we can and there's no need for you to make a final judgment.

"He was disappointed in his career, Ducks," Billy told me that night, getting in a little meaningless grope. "And in his love life. Wife left him for another broad. And with his kiddies who all detest the bastard. Ignore the wretch is my advice." As long as he ignores me, I told Billy, taking his claw of a hand off my butt and putting it back where it belonged.

I had given them a good show, even if I say so myself. They were, after all, nice people. I went around as I usually do and shook all the guys' hands and buzzed the ladies on their over made-up cheeks and then, out of the corner of my eye what do I see but this bastard staring at me as he liked to do at Trucks.

It was as if he had poison daggers in his eyes and they were focusing on me. I couldn't help myself. I went right up to him and said, "Listen, man, I have nothing against you and I don't see why you have to be such a dick. I've shaken every guy's hand on this board. C'mon. Let's be friends."

I don't think I've ever seen so much hate in another person's face. It seemed to ooze out of his wrinkles. He pushed my hand away with as much strength as he could get up, spilling his plastic cup of cheap Scotch as he did so, his whole body shaking with anger. "I don't shake hands with fags," he said with all that venom, spit coming out of his mouth. "Fag," he said again. Everyone stopped talking. "Fag, fag, fag."

Billy put on a tape. "It's Raining Men," by RuPaul, of all songs, and he put his arm around my shoulder and walked me to the further end of the May-Be and told me to stow it, the guy's a creepy creep, not long for this world — neither was Billy, for that matter — and anyway, Miss May-Be was docking.

It was all over. Billy thought.

The writers and their pals moved up the plank, not looking at the Creepy Creep but saying goodbye to me, a few of them handing me extra tips for what I guess I had went through. They were all embarrassed. Billy said he had to get home; he had a fearful need to have a bowel movement; the little scene had made his tummy all nervous.

That left the Creep and me. He was, as usual, staring at me. It was getting dark, the water was electric blue, the famous green ghost reflection of the sun was just sitting on the horizon, and then plump, it went down.

"How much?" the Creep said and I knew instantly just what he wanted.

"A million bucks plus tip. I wouldn't let you touch me."

He stood up and made for the plank, whispering in his whiskey voice, "Fag, fag, fag."

He was all stooped over, looking like the pope coming out his airplane in Syria. "Fag, fag, fag."

His butt, big as the moon in old green shorts, faced me as he tried to maneuver up the plank. I swear it, I couldn't stop myself. I kicked him as hard as I could with my foot. His head hit the tip of the plank leaving a little blood on the old wood. He rolled over and fell face down into the shallow water, sinking into the mud, finally, disappearing.

I stuck a pole down there in the water where I thought his back might be to see if there was any movement. If he showed signs of life, I might have tried to pull him out. Just to save my ass. But there was no movement whatsoever. I put the pole back aboard the Little Miss May-Be, locked up and hustled. I had to go home first and change if I was going to take my place on the meat rack at Trucks.

I realized, of course, that Creepy was talking about himself with his last words. I said them over my shoulder into the wind as I undid my bike and sped off toward the Rue Royale.

SILVER

ROSALIND BRACKENBURY

It was past midsummer. The red flowers of the royal poinciana lay and drifted, a mat upon the surface of the water. A slight wind moved the mat back and forth, made ripples happen, dappled the bottom of the pool with bright rings and shadow. I was alone here, mid-afternoon, my feet in the water and the rest of me dripping from my swim. The huge tree overhead loosed a few more petals. Scarlet upon blue water. The sky between branches a deep blue, the leaves still pale green, nothing ruined yet or lost. Somebody moved inside the house but didn't come outside. I moved my feet and felt water skim my ankles, warm, almost as warm as blood.

I'd said I'd go up to see her this afternoon. Imagined the crack of the heat and the glare of it on traffic this afternoon, the glass and metal, blacktop, the hardness we've made of this world, which once was soft, swampy, regenerative. It's not far up the Keys, but you'd rather be here with your feet in a blue pool than tackle that traffic and be thinking what to say when you got there, and what to do. Anybody would.

On a summer afternoon, you don't feel like thinking about death. So maybe I wouldn't think about it, I'd just go, like I'd go to see anybody, and just visit, and be there, and not have it be anything special. I'd take her some of this outside world. A flower, this warmth on my skin. She wouldn't want chlorine, or the false blue of a pool.

The reality is, we're all dying; it's just a matter of time. And anybody who isn't actually dead is living. There isn't a halfway state. So maybe this stuff about visiting the dying is just mine, my fear of finding something shocking, something I hadn't expected. Maybe this is what everyone who visits her thinks. Maybe if you're in that state, you just long for someone to ignore it, talk to you as if you were going to be there forever.

"I just thought I'd call in. No special reason, no."

We think about it a lot, because there's a lot of it going on. You can't help noticing. It's like drawing lots, over and over again, and breathing out with relief to find it isn't you. Some people spend a lot of time and attention trying to find reasons. You didn't live right, eat right, didn't look after yourself enough, didn't think the right way. So the person who's sick and maybe dying also has to feel guilty about not having lived the right way. Nobody can stand the arbitrariness of it. A cell, suddenly in revolt. A collapse inward. It's easier to conceive of blame.

My friend Silver has lived an extraordinary life. She's been in jail and on hunger strike, she's marched and sat down and been beaten and feigned death on many occasions. She's acted according to her beliefs — a rare thing, these days of contingency, these times of selfishness. She's fought racism and sexism and the oppression of gays, and she's been there protesting while rockets went up loaded with plutonium and while bombs dropped on people in Iraq; she's organized the buying and sharing of land in these land-hungry decades, while Florida's been chopped and shaved and laid out like a corpse in a morgue; and she's a lesbian. I'm not, but I can see that for her it's logical. It's being out there, visible and vulnerable, afraid yet brave, all the things I am not and do not do. I sit by a swimming pool in Old Town on a summer afternoon and I think about her life, and all it has meant. Then I get up and put shorts and T-shirt quickly over my swimsuit while I'm still wet, and get my car keys out of my pocket, and go.

She's in bed, in a room that has been prepared for her by women. There are paintings and cards pinned up all over the walls, and flowers in vases and cartoons and children's drawings, and photographs of women. There are always women in attendance. Some of them are from Texas, Arkansas, Boston, New York. She's famous, powerful; she wants them and they come. In the movie made of her life, they had small parts. Some of them are ex-lovers. Some are women who had quarrels with her long ago and have come here to make up, before it is too late. Two of them are here this afternoon; one smooths her sheet, the other brings in fruit on a plate. She turns her face away, grimaces at me. Slices of mango and banana, cut thin. Grapes, cut in half so the pips show.

"I can't eat."

I find a chair and pull it to the bedside. She motions me to the other side, where it's easier for her to turn her head to me. Her body isn't working; she has to obey its will, and so must everyone. She is not, has never been easy. It may be this lack of easiness that has let her survive this long.

Her eyes upon me, that steadfast still-bright blue. I think again how the flesh falls away from faces and shows the starkness of their architecture, the remorseless bone-truth of what has made them. Her hair is brushed, short and completely white. Her skin is smoothed over the bone. She smiles at me and I hope it is not an effort. The other women, like nurses, with that subservient air people take around her, leave us alone.

She says, "Well, hello, Ms. Annie. You have to be dying to get air-conditioning round here, see?" The AC cools the room so my sweat cools and dries on me uncomfortably. Outside, raucous and fierce as ever, the Florida midsummer afternoon, crickets and mosquitoes, ticks and frogs, the ceaseless click and whirr, the heat, the sharp grass, the plants that sting. And mangoes heavy in the trees and plopping down with their sudden thud, and papaya, avocados like little grenades; and half-naked women passing between the trees they've planted here. It's Silver's place, her dream. Only she could never let it be, once it was created, and still she lies here fretting, about meetings, and decisions, and documents to be signed, before she can let go. Will she let go? Should one, and go gracefully, or fight, and hold on? Nobody knows. The culture of death is among us, and we don't know its rules.

She says, "I have something to say to you. Can you just listen?"

"Yes."

"I've had enough. I want to die."

I say nothing. I hold her hand, feel the pulse beat and the slight tremor of fingers.

With all the starvation and mockery and imprisonment, she's never before given in. She was Joan of Arc, Boadicea, she was Amazon. But is this giving in, or simply going on to the next stage? As in protests, where the next stage is an arrest; arrests, where the next stage is jail. I think of her as a person who threw herself into the vast machinery of society which like an ocean liner was set on a particular course. One twist of the wheel would never be enough to change its course one jot; no, but ten miles on, with enough pressure, it will change. What Silver has done will have its effect, but down the line, not yet.

After a very long silence, I say, "It's okay."

"I've tried. I've tried everything they suggested, I thought I still had work to do, and should do my utmost to live. I can't. You know," and her hand gripped mine more strongly, "There comes a time when the pain is much stronger, it just takes over. I never knew it before. But there is something stronger than we are. And it's that."

She said, "Write. Will you? That's what you can do."

It was the last time I saw her, that late June afternoon, before the summer turned. I said goodbye to the other women, some of whom were crying. I walked, half-blinded, to my car. What was the logic of it? She lived her life for others — for freedom, justice, equality, in these times which care so little for these things. She fought her way through them, right up to the end. She spent her life in battle. Her death came too early. Her anger was at all the things which were wrong, the injustices, the lies. Was it the anger which consumed her? While I was lying by pools, reading, watching the sun blot the branches of the royal poinciana, she was fighting. Her last fight was with cancer. It looked like the pain was what won. But who can tell, where pain ends and there is glory, and what it looks like, a place without strife, and whether we should ever desire it?

Outside her house, in the commune that women have made, grass grows long and quickly, the Brazilian pepper reaches back everywhere unless you cut it, the wood of the little houses is eaten by termites and broken up easily by wind and rain. The earth is soft and loose here, it's springy and swampy, nobody's covered it over with asphalt or driven in posts or concrete slabs. The earth is left to be itself. It's been bought, like a freed slave, it's free in perpetuity, because of Silver and the land trust she organized and worked for until she became too sick. The women who live here know how to mourn. They know the rituals. Ash from old fires mingles in wet earth. Bodies are buried here, reduced to ash, and the cycles go on, buttonwood and poisonwood, elephant's ear and philodendron, tough Florida grass, women's tongue.

The last time I drove up there, a rainbow had one end in the women's village and the other in the ocean. A steel blue arch of sky in between, gold where sun hit the water, rain in diagonals. And everything grows and grows, the plants of Florida will push up and crack concrete given time; and time is all we need.

Leaf Woman

MARGIT BISZTRAY

Madeline opens the door to her house and to a day without plans. If anyone has earned a day off, it is Madeline. And now, at eight-fifteen a.m., it's time for Madeline's Day-Off-Activity-List, item one. Though it's an actual list, written in dying, blue pen, it doesn't mean she has plans. It isn't that kind of list. It has no structure, no appointments. It's easy-going. The list only suggests things, which serve as bumpers to coax her back into the flow if she gets stalled and starts wasting her time. Catch a few rays. Observe the sunset. Sip cocktail while listening to long-haired guitar artist.

She really wants the day to flow, as in be fluid and relaxing, but also continuously moving. This will make the most of her free time, because she's out of practice in the use of free time. This is the first day off she's had in fifty-six days, not counting the half-day she spent in the emergency room when Rudy cut off his thumb instead of chopping a lamb shank. She'd been the only employee who knew how to drive a stick, and she'd driven crazily, weaving through traffic on Roosevelt as if Rudy's life were at stake.

"Slow down," he kept repeating. "Christ, you're gonna get me there in pieces. Take me back and use the knife, okay? It'd be cheaper."

But Madeline is out of practice in slowing down. Sometimes she feels like those mechanics at the racetrack, who run wielding the tools to change the tire, spin things around, pump the machine, then get the hell out of the way so that the engines can roar again. She is the driver as well, and maybe even the car. She moved to Key West to live the island life, which she'd imagined as one of flip-flops and floppy straw hats, the Summer section at WalMart. Sometimes she does wear plastic flip-flops to the Information Booth, so she can wiggle her untanned feet to Jimmy Buffett and watch the tan tourists pass. It makes her feel jaunty, and a tad sarcastic.

"For your information, I can't afford to give directions unless you tip me."

"For your information, I have a college degree in Biology. I'm not an idiot. Which for your information cannot be said of you."

"Hemingway? Yeah, he had a house here. He's dead now."

Tapping her feet to Jimmy Buffett, Madeline smiles, answers the questions the proper way and hands out a map.

Before her shift ends, she changes into sprinting shoes so she can sprint to her job at the seafood emporium and serve people too much fried food.

"For your information, that's a lot of cholesterol." Oops, wrong job. "Today's fresh catch is mahi-mahi. The chef's conch chowder is excellent."

On her day off, she'll wear the flip-flops and get one of those pedicures with sequins. Maybe she'll buy herself a toe ring! Anything's possible; or, at least she hopes so. She hopes it's possible for her. She's set her sights on this day so many times, she is afraid it will cancel her. "Sorry, I've found someone more qualified. You can go back to work, Madeline Smith." At seven-thirty in the morning, Rudy called. He's been promoted to manager since no one else has showed up as faithfully as he did. "Want to work for Jill?" he asked. "She partied late last night." Madeline snorted and hung up the phone.

She'll read The Citizen all the way through. She settles into the seat of her porch glider — so, it is a glider! — and peeks at the newspaper's headlines. Chickens to be relocated to the indigenous park, although not indigenous. Residents sick of torn-up roads. Everglades burning up north, highway still closed. Well, that's good news for the Governor, since now there will be less park to protect, Madeline thinks. With this thought a surge of resentment strikes, not for the Governor alone, but for those who voted him in, and those who didn't vote at all. She hasn't thought about politics in ages, which is an easy accomplishment for those who hand out maps and fried food all day.

Her horoscope offers the usual weak broth: a deed will prove unfruitful, a friend will bring change. There is the movie schedule, should she see a movie? Or, should she buy magazines and catch up on fashion and gossip and the arts? No, she should do something more soulful, like sit beside the ocean reading Kahil Gibran. She ought to cook something nutritious! Perhaps this day off is all a bad idea. She can't seem to do it right. She ought to work and take a long vacation later.

"Hi there."

A man has suddenly appeared at her gate. He looks familiar. Maybe she's waited on him.

"I'm Jake. I live next door. We've never said hello."

Briefly she remembers someone like him moving her trash cans to the curb once. Does he perhaps wear a uniform to work? She thinks so.

"I have been meaning to ask if I can take some Key limes off you. They're perfect right now, unless you have plans for them of course."

She sees he means the yellow orbs making a mess of her yard. The tree is almost chartreuse with more.

"Sure, help yourself," she says.

"Thanks! They make the yummiest margaritas. And of course, Key lime pie, and great ceviche and limeade. A lot of things."

Apparently, these things are edible. The pie sold at the seafood emporium comes frozen from Texas, so how was she supposed to know Key limes were actual fruit, the French fries aren't from France! Jake removes his t-shirt and makes a sling of it.

"Come for margaritas, neighbor!"

"Oh, no thanks. Today, no plans."

He smiles crookedly. "Okay. When you have plans, come by."

She's out of practice in social skills. She can't make simple conversation! Perhaps she's insecure. She ought to take one of those quizzes. It bothers her that two new people have stopped outside her fence and one is pointing at her.

"We were admiring the gingerbread," the woman says, catching her eye. "The turtles over the seagrass. Unusual. Do you know the story?"

Madeline pivots her head. Lo and behold, her porch is trimmed with swimming turtles.

"We saw a turtle on the way to Fort Jefferson. Wasn't that magical, honey?"

The man strokes the woman's arm. They are no doubt on their honeymoon. Madeline sees this type of couple a lot: late-blooming honeymooners. Couples in their forties, newly in love. She has a theory about them. They've had to look harder and wait longer, so they will try harder and last longer. They accept that they are two complete people, whereas the younger couples still seem to want to be exactly alike. "Don't get the ice cream," the young wife or girlfriend says, "Get the sorbet." Late-bloomers order the ice cream, share it, then order seconds. Smiling, they joke about soft waistlines and getting to the gym someday. She really hopes to stay single and be a late-bloomer.

"Have a nice day!" she calls. The couple waves, and in the instant they turn and walk away, a man on a bicycle throws Madeline a mango. She catches it, stunned. He turns in the middle of the street and throws another into her lap. Then, he bikes away. She holds a mango to her nose. It smells like pine needles and canned, Mandarin oranges. It smells like bee pollen.

"They are related to poison ivy, just so you know."

"What?"

She'll go inside if people don't leave her alone starting right now.

"Yes ma'm, and cashews. People who pick cashews die. The poison seeps into their bodies and kills em'." He holds his hands in front of him, puts on invisible gloves. "Don't put the skin close to your mouth, is all. Might get a rash."

He's old and homeless and obviously crazy. He bends over a luggage cart piled with folded newspapers. A rickety, folded chair is strapped on top. The white undershirt he wears is limp and stretched like a stocking, exposing his concave torso.

"Me and my wife owned a beauty school. Called it the Southernmost Beauty School. She hated mangoes." He pats the chair. "It's time for us to sit and read the news. Have a nice day." He waves goodbye, then trundles off, dragging his luggage cart. Madeline cradles the mangoes, one in each hand. Their skin is cool to the touch, but with an underlying warmth, like a baby's shoulder.

"That guy's a millionaire," a voice says.

Madeline had always imagined she lived on a quiet street. Now it's like she is a tollbooth, only she's not making a dime. Screw it, it's time to go inside. The woman walking six miniature dogs will not stop talking. "It's true! He owns the house with the spiral stairs? The blue tiled tower? Birdbath? Hasn't got kids, either. A shame."

The dogs drag her away, talking still. "Hoped he might donate . . . a dog shelter."

"Clean up that mess!" Madeline watches a stream of blond hair flow by. "Get back and clean that shit up!" There is commotion and the hair streams by again, followed by a plastic bag opened to look like a parachute.

"You lazy DOG LADY!" the hair screams. It stops outside Madeline's gate. "Don't you loathe dog shit? Fuck it — who doesn't loathe dog shit!" She sees a frustrated, feminine man. He leans before her and pants, pressing his hand to his chest like a bony squid.

"I stay up too late for this! But I've been watching that dog lady. I knew her dogs shit on my sidewalk, knew it! Oh god, I broke a nail. Got any Crazy Glue?"

Madeline nods. Using the utmost care, he slides open her gate latch. "Thank God. Could you please get it?" He arranges himself on her front steps. He doesn't seem to be going away. In fact, he's whimpering, as if on the verge of pain. He wouldn't last long in the wild.

As he is patching his nail, he spies the mangoes, which rolled under the glider. "Is that a Haden? Oh I just love Hadens! Bring one, I need one now."

Madeline obeys, hoping he'll soon leave her alone.

"It smells like honeysuckle! Like apricots! I could just die!" He takes it in his good hand and holds it like a marble, admiring the sunset skin. She's never seen a person look this hard at anything. He sighs and puts it down.

She holds it out to him. "Take it."

"Really? Oh really, really?"

She really hopes he won't cry.

"My former lover could only eat mangoes when he was dying. I cut them up for him. I got a rash, but it was something I could do. So I just did it." He bends his face over the mango. "Thank you. And thanks for the Crazy Glue. You saved my life."

Her porch seems suddenly quiet. Leaves of The Citizen riffle, then blow away. Two swallowtails rise and dip and rise, as if suspended on elastic. Their wings resemble puzzle pieces, trying to fit together. Two lizards pause on her railing, under the turtles and seagrass, like some Darwinian diagram. They spread their throats apart like fans, then dart into the Key lime tree. Everything travels in twos, in matched sets. This realization depressed her when she got here, before the late-bloomers proved that being loveable has no expiration date. Madeline smiles. She knows, without great effort, without expense, that she has cured an old pain. Somewhere, during her racetrack-like days, she has been fixed. How many ways has she been fixed? She's been too busy to count or even notice. How many times has she missed mangoes tossed right into her lap?

She's sitting still. Briefly, she wonders if this means the flow has stalled. Should she consult the Activity List? Or, another voice says, she could just sit and glide a few more moments. She glides, and many moments pass.

The sun begins to hum with intensity. She really ought to get a suntan, but then she's noticing the leaves around her lengthening with heat, audibly green as they build chlorophyll and change it into oxygen. She takes a deep breath, thanking the plants for the gift of life. This isn't like her: she studied Biology in college! The heat is having an effect. Soon she'll be dragging a luggage cart piled high with newspapers. That man was normal once too, and now look at him. It's just, the leaves make this incredible noise! She feels she's inside the foliage now, not as in a cage: as in an actual, green body. She's turning into a leaf-woman. She can't go back to work tomorrow. Leaf women do not sit inside! They do not hand out fried clams! Leaf women glide. Leaf women wind around the porch spindles into the gingerbread, where turtles swim.

"Knock-knock! Your margarita! Room service!"

Jake has returned, carrying a glass shaped like a cactus. She is relieved, and then surprised at her relief.

"These leaves are so amazing," Madeline says. She hasn't moved. She can't stop gliding.

"Oh yeah!" Jake's eyes are round. "Like when the sun gets hot, they make that click-click sound?"

He chants a low, mournful thrum, like she has only heard monks on PBS do.

She laughs. Is everyone in Key West insane from too much chlorophyll? Is this why people take time off? She takes the cactus and tips it to her mouth. The drink tastes light as a butterfly, dainty as a honeysuckle dipped into brine. It tastes chartreuse.

"Thank you," she says, after a moment of tasting. "I can't believe those limes have been here all along. I'm so embarrassed for wasting them."

Jake brushes away her words, then waves her goodbye. She sits awhile with the sour and salt, and then she starts to crave more flavors. She craves the flavors she's smelled biking to work, the quick perceptions she's passed. There is the Cuban paella she's never tried, the place that sells crepes with warm jam, the place that hisses with warm, barbecue smoke. She'd like a pineapple smoothie, a slice of real Key lime pie, one of those jerk chicken sandwiches that pricks her nose with clove. First, she'd like a mango. She'd like to cut the sunset slivers and really, truly taste them. Then she'll call Rudy and tell him how sick she is.

"I'm sick of living like a racetrack."

"I'm sick of fried food and fake Key lime pie."

"I'm sick and tired of this life."

"And for the information of you at the Information Booth, I'll be retiring now."

She's going to pick up the phone and call Rudy now. She's going to call him, after she glides a moment longer.

Corrida Faux Pas

WILLIAM WILLIAMSON

"Goddamn, that was fucking awesome," Corky said. Suddenly pounding the dashboard once with his fist. Cat was sitting between us. She flinched like she'd been shocked by a snafu of electricity. I'd just turned right off Truman Avenue onto Duval Street. Years ago the locals dubbed Duval Street the longest street in the world because it ran from the Gulf of Mexico to the Atlantic Ocean. From one side of Key West to the other. A staggering two whole miles. But at times a two-mile carnival of tropical decadence. A stew of carnal sights, foreign sounds and a potpourri of tantalizing smells. Sometimes the Duval crawl slowed down to a sensory overload. Then it becomes a banquet of de rigeur promiscuity.

I thought that maybe Corky had seen another hip-shaking, ass-swinging woman lighting up the sidewalk. One that I missed. Punching the dash like he did. Key West was inundated with cheesecake some days. Bodies walking just to be seen. Noticed. Whistled at. Wolfed at. I glanced quickly out of the corner of my eye, looking to see if Corky was going to explain himself any further. Caught myself looking down at Cat's knees pinched together beside me. Her kneecaps were so thin and pale they resembled light bulbs.

"What?" Cat blurted. She turned her head left and right wondering what she was missing.

Cat was intrigued with Key West like most first time visitors. She'd been here once before and the enchantment of the island had stayed with her. Something about the quaint town stuck to her like washed up tar on the beach. I could feel her melting a little more. Softening. Succumbing to Key West's charms.

"I was thinking about that octopus in the bucket back at your place, Henry. I still can't believe it," Corky shouted over the steel drum music on the radio. Jimmy Buffet's latest bankroll. I turned it down.

"I got up before either one of you this morning and it was still kind of dark. I went over to the table to sit down but before I did, I looked down in the bucket to see if that octopus was still in there. He was all balled up like he was sleeping. Those two tropical fish were swimming around him like they didn't have a thing to worry about. The next thing I know, while I'm standing there watching, the octopus flings himself at one of the fish. Wrapped his tentacles around that little fucker and smothered him like stink on shit!"

"That fish didn't have a chance! It was all over in a second. What did you say those fish were called?" Corky asked.

"They're Sergeant Majors," I told him. "Or were," I added. Corky wasn't exaggerating. I knew exactly what he meant. Like stink on shit. Didn't have a chance.

"Yeah, well, he got his ass ate. Majorly, by that octopus. You should've seen it, Cat. Turn the radio back up," Corky said, reaching for the dial.

"No, leave it down. I gotta look for a place to park," I told him.

"I'm glad I didn't see it," Cat admitted. She wrinkled her nose with an unpleasant look on her face. Recrossed her light bulbs.

I fished a cigarette out of a pack from the front pocket of my shirt. Felt for my lighter in my pants pocket.

"Remember, I wanted to let them go. Down at the dock behind Henry's house," Cat reminded us.

"The other fish, the Sergeant Major that was left, started going absolutely nuts in the bucket. Darting around in circles. I think he knew his ass was next," Corky said excitedly.

"He's next, but not today," I told him.

"What do you mean?" Cat asked with her eyes open wide. Full of concern.

"The octopus will get him, but not today. He'll wait for tomorrow night. That's how octopuses are. They get hungry and are aggressive and kill for a meal but they're not greedy. The Sergeant Major that's left will be on the menu tomorrow night."

Cat elbowed me in the ribs causing me to almost sideswipe a parked car.

"Jesus Christ! What was that for?"

"Henry! You jerk! You knew that octopus was going to stalk those poor reef fish and eat them and you just left them in that bucket for that hideous, looking, looking...that hideous thing!" Cat scolded me. Her eyebrows penciled upwards.

"What else could I do?" I asked facetiously.

"Let the damn poor things go. Like I wanted to do. Let them go in the water behind your house. At least they would of had a chance," she whined.

I shrugged. Found my lighter, lit my cigarette. A chance. That's all we really have in life is a chance. Took a right on Southard Street and found a place to park that still had forty-five minutes on the meter.

I was almost twice Corky's age. He was eighteen years old. All testosterone and hormones. Come hell or high water he was determined to meet Jake for the first time. After my mom divorced Jake, she left Matecumbe and moved to the mainland. She had all she could take of my dad's drinking, his womanizing and the Keys.

Six months after she moved, she gave birth prematurely to Corky in the backseat of a car at a drive-in theater. I asked her what movie the theater was showing but she didn't remember. She was by herself. Almost hemorrhaged to death till someone found her after the drive-in closed.

For eighteen years Corky was my half-brother. Mom said his father was some man she had met at a bar. Never saw him again. I believed her. Till yesterday. When Corky showed up unexpectedly at my door demanding to know why I never told him about Jake. Cat was with him. I'd never seen her before. Corky picked her up along the way. She was hitchhiking to Key West with him. Mom had finally told Corky the truth about Jake after all these years. It was news to me. Jake was Corky's father. I didn't know what to believe. Who to believe.

Jake wasn't anywhere to be found in three of the bars on Duval that I knew he liked to hang out in. Either he wasn't there or the latest bartender of the month didn't know him. Or they acted like they did know him but they didn't know where he might be found. Bartenders down in Key West change jobs like flies change directions. Like a woman changes underwear. And the good bartenders that do stick around for any length of time know not to divulge too much information about someone else's business with strangers. It was best that way. I was indifferent to their help anyway. Maybe they did know where Jake was and maybe they didn't. I knew eventually, I would find Jake and introduce Corky to him.

"Hey, Jake, here's the son you didn't know you had." What happened after that was out of my hands. I was only the messenger. Somehow, though, I felt as the harbinger, I was going to get my wings broke.

A woman named Tony that I vaguely knew at The Bull Whistle told us Jake had been there the day before. He wasn't drunker than hell and he'd left a lousy tip so Tony figured Jake was in between jobs. Money slipped through Jake's fingers like water through a shrimp net. When Jake came off the boat with a pocket full of money he liked to spend it freely. Easily. Jake had an insouciant attitude towards money. Always did. Money was easy come, easy go to him. Practically giving it away in tips. Plying women and friends with rounds of drinks. Especially women. Even if he knew it wouldn't get him anywhere. Jake called it the twelve-pack ratio. Buy twelve different women drinks at twelve different times and invariably, luck would swing his way. In the pendulum of odds, one of the women might sleep with him.

We lingered for a while on the sidewalk outside The Bull Whistle. Taking in the street life and tourists strolling by. I was trying to decide what to do next. Two grunge rock looking teenagers stopped and tried to get Corky to buy Cat a flower they'd made by meticulously folding a palm frond sliver till it resembled a rose bud. Sidewalk origami. Corky didn't buy it and Cat didn't seem to care one way or the other. The two kids walked away to try and find some other gullible tourist to sell their dime store artwork to. I was glad that Corky turned them down. There were too many peddlers down here trying to make a dollar by calling themselves artists in Key West. Some of the peddlers on Duval were no more than two legged roaches scavenging for any crumbs they could subsist on. Their only real talent was staying alive without any talent. Clutching the simpatico purse strings of hope.

A new act started performing on the stage behind us in The Bull Whistle. We turned around. Watched the show looking through the large, open windows. Standing in front of a row of planter boxes trailing purple bougainvillaea down to the sidewalk.

It took Cat's insistence and at least fifteen minutes of complete mesmerized disbelief before Corky allowed himself to accept the stark reality. The women up on the stage dressed up like the Supremes, jiving and chorusing to the melody of, "Stop! In The Name Of Love," were actually men. Drag queens. Having fun. Putting on a show.

"But they're all gorgeous, " Corky stammered, justifying his skepticism.

I had to agree. They did look good. The meticulous attention the performers had put in their make-up and costumes made them appear as attractive and sensual looking to watch as any real group of women.

"Look at their calves, dummy. That's the dead give away," Cat pointed out. She was right. Their calf muscles were diamond-shaped. Too muscular for a woman.

"I know. I know. I believe you, but I don't believe it," he said shaking his head with a mixture of regret and doubt.

"Get a load of these two," I mumbled under my breath to Corky.

He turned and looked down the sidewalk. Coming towards us from a block away, walking in an awkward high-heeled gait, were two blatant, flaming queens. Sashaying their gaudy presence for all it was worth. On parade. From where we stood it was apparent the two hadn't quite mastered the delicate walk of a woman in high heels. Their knees were buckling and their ankles kept threatening to turn inwards. They both wore flamboyant, scarlet mini dresses with sequins and both carried white purses clutched in their manly, gnarly fingers. Neither one of them had bothered to shave their legs. One even had a thin mustache, further supporting that their flagrant charade was just that. A charade. They didn't care. They were happy to be sugar stepping.

To me they looked like what they were. Drag queen clowns. A pathetic parody of a woman and nothing else. One of the queens' breasts was grossly disproportionate to the other breast. And his silver wig was seated so crookedly on his head that the disparity was both comic and sad. Both of their faces were hideously overdone in lashes, mascara and stop sign red lipstick. They smiled at us before they went into The Bull Whistle.

"Jesus Christ, they must be fifty or sixty years old," Corky commented.

I raised my eyebrows. Let out a short laugh.

"Just think. They could be some kid's grandfather," I suggested.

"Oh, my God! That's terrible!" Cat chimed and made a wrinkled face that made Corky and me both laugh.

Something sparked in me. I immediately felt a brotherly, blood connection to Corky because we were both laughing with the same degrading sense of humor. It occurred to me that maybe I felt good about the sudden realization was because I was gaining a family member, instead of losing one or distancing myself away from another. That was something new for me. Corky was my real blood brother. Not a half brother like mom had claimed all these years. Till yesterday. Imagine that. I wondered why the deception.

I thought since we were already downtown and if Corky wanted to know about his ancestors on Jake's side of the family and try to solidify the past he felt he was missing, we might as well visit the cemetery and the family plot on Windsor Lane. The only piece of real estate in Key West I could afford to live at. If I wanted to be stacked on top of some of my ancestors when I died. Which I didn't. I led them walking down Angela Street to the graveyard.

The cemetery needed mowing. Actually, the cemetery needed a lot of things. Some attention reserved for the dead for one. The grass was parched and sick looking from the lack of any rain recently. Water was too expensive to irrigate the grass. V-shaped seed stalks wavered knee high like an abandoned wheat field. Weeds grew in abundant clusters between the rows of headstones on either side of us. You could sense the pain this ground held. See the suffering neglect of concrete and heritage decaying with age. Feel the importance of ancestors long since departed but unfortunately long forgotten.

Corky and Cat saw the timeless neglect of the past as well. Some of the graves were crumbling. Leaving soft piles of dust in the corners. The dust drifted in the air like flower pollen when the breeze picked up. Some of the graves that were set in the ground were caving in. Every direction was a sea of decrepit tombs resting on top of the ground. Key West couldn't bury their dead in the ground because of the low salt water table below the soil. Even the palm trees, with their tattered fronds, seemed frail and dying.

"This place is a wreck," Corky said looking around.

"Yeah," Cat agreed. Her steps were cautious. One paw at a time like a feline.

It was true. Death is never pretty. And graveyards are never a Monet landscape. In any shape, color or form. But what did these dead people care, I had to ask myself? It's the generation after them that should be ashamed for forgetting them.

It had been a while since the last time I'd visited the cemetery in Key West. The dead spoke to you in immortal whispers with their dates and short synapses of their life spent on the Rock, etched in fading stone. My thoughts were rambling. I was putting something out of my mind. Something bothered me in this cemetery. Something always came back and haunted me here.

We walked down the narrow lane heading towards the Catholic section of the cemetery. The blacktop was potholed in spots and spider webbed with cracks from enduring centuries of the fierce Key West sun. I heard car tires rolling behind us and looked back. Two Monroe County cops were slowly creeping up behind us. The lane was just wide enough for a single car to pass so we stepped into the grass between two leaning headstones and let them pass.

Up ahead was an old Cuban man wearing a floppy straw hat and a sleeveless undershirt. He was stooped over standing next to a garbage can with weeds in it that he'd been lethargically pulling. Motioning with his hands towards the cops and pointing deeper into the rows of graves and vaults that blanketed the cemetery.

The two cops passed by us in their patrol cars. Both of them were craning their necks to get a look at us behind their mirrored sunglasses.

"What do you think is going on?" Corky asked.

"No telling. I don't see any funeral going on so I don't think they are funeral escorts or here to direct traffic. Maybe the caretaker found the remains of some chicken or goat the Cubans sacrificed last night." I wasn't totally serious but it happens in Key West.

"Sacrificed?" Cat asked. "You mean like voodoo?"

"Yeah. Some of the Cubans and Haitians on the island worship a religion called Santeria. Sometimes they sneak into the cemetery at night, decorate some grave like an altar with candles, fruit, shells and other shit and sacrifice a chicken or a goat to the spirits. Or whatever the hell they believe in."

"That's sick," Cat said disgustingly. "Ghoulish." Her shoulders shivered at the thought.

"What do they do, cut the chicken's head off or something?" Corky wanted to know.

"Yea, something like that."

I looked up. A turkey vulture flew over. Circled the cemetery.

"Sometimes they draw pentagrams and strange symbols in animal blood. And leave chicken legs and beaks and other ornaments around a grave after they've finished."

"Why?" Corky asked.

"Who knows? Why do the Catholics let priests put communion wafers on their tongues to eat, calling them the blood of Christ? If you're asking me to explain religion, then you're asking the wrong person."

"That's too weird for me," Cat said. I could've sworn there was a trace of arousal in her voice.

"Well, we can turn around. Makes no difference to me. What do you want to do, Corky?" I asked. I was ready to leave as soon as I walked under the cemetery's ornate iron gates.

"I want to see the graves," he said.

We kept walking. But with a slower, curious purpose in our minds and steps. Wondering what we might find amongst the dead. I decided after we leave the cemetery, I would drive back over to Stock Island to see if Jake was there yet. He lived on a shrimp boat. He wasn't on the boat when we stopped by earlier. If he still wasn't there, I'd stop by Scary Gary's trailer. He might know where Jake was. Scary Gary had his own small network of cronies that fed him information. And I wanted to buy a bag of grass. Scary Gary always had good grass.

The two patrol cars that passed us stopped up ahead. The officers got out. Hitched their gun belts higher over their big, rolling asses. Walked over to the old Cuban caretaker. I don't know what it is about cops and the leather gun holsters they wear, but when they strap their holsters on, they all walk differently. With a gunslinger's swagger.

The two officers talked to the old man briefly and left him standing by his trash can. They walked deeper into the confusion of tombstones and pillbox-like vaults. They disappeared behind a white mausoleum that was built a hundred and fifty years ago for one of the richer families on the island. A naked, but featureless marble angel was perched on the roof guarding the entrance.

We could see that the two cops had stopped walking. They were looking down. Talking. Gesturing. A few seconds later a woman stood up. All we could see was her head. Rising like a spirit from below the plain of graves.

As we came up behind the police cars the old caretaker looked up. He grinned sheepishly at us. The three of us stopped. Presently the cops reemerged from behind the mausoleum with a butt ass naked woman between them. Corky and me looked at each other. We looked at Cat. Her mouth was open in shock.

"She's naked," Cat announced.

She was naked. A very blond, very beautiful, very butt ass naked woman, I wanted to add. Her caramel skin stood out from the ubiquitous, fading white and gray of the cemetery like a full moon in the night sky.

The naked woman was a statuesque goddess. A smiling vixen that arose from the graves like a phoenix. She was tall and regal with legs up to her neck. She seemed to diminish the two cops escorting her. Her pendulous breasts rose and swung in stride. A mane of golden hair showered her back down to her waist. When she got closer to us, I could see her skin was flawless. Not a tan line anywhere to be seen and she had the daintiest, lightest strip of downy pubic hair I'd ever seen grace a woman.

"Holy shit," Corky whispered, staring indiscriminately. I couldn't blame him. None of us could take our eyes off of her. We were speechless. It was like watching an apparition or an angel materializing before your eyes from out of the ground. A free spirit walking across water. Walking through a sea of graves. Cat had her palm to her mouth in awe.

The goddess was carrying a pile of clothes and a paperback book clutched to her stomach. She was wearing a whimsical smile on her face. Clearly the woman wasn't embarrassed by her nakedness or being caught in flagrante delicto either. The two cops were hiding behind their sunglasses. But it was evident to me by the motion of their heads that they were thoroughly enjoying checking her out from head to toe as they guided her to the patrol car by her elbows.

"Why don't they let her put her clothes back on?" Cat wondered.

Corky and I didn't say anything. We were transfixed. Lost in the surreal reality of it all. Like finding a stranger sleeping in your bed. Wondering how? Why? Who the hell is this? Besides, I knew the Bubbas escorting her was enjoying the show. Something to brag about at the station while they rubbed their balls.

The officers led the naked woman to one of the cars. Opened the back door, put a hand on her head, bent her down and directed her inside. From the rear window we watched her toss her hair from her eyes like an agitated lioness. The cops turned back to the caretaker. Spoke to him briefly. He bobbed his head up and down several times in agreement and shrugged his shoulders. One of the officers gave the old man a playful punch to the shoulder, and then they turned away. Walked to their respective cars and drove off.

"What was that all about?" I asked when we walked up to the caretaker. He took a red handkerchief out of his back pocket. Dappled his forehead and cheeks nervously.

"She was out there sunbathing on her dead husband's grave," he told us. His teeth were small and rotten like black, Halloween candy corn. "She has piles of money but she doesn't have all her oars in the water. I told her before, this is a family cemetery and I would call the cops if I caught her doing it again."

"You've seen her out here naked before?" Cat asked.

"Before? Oh yes, many, many times. I don't know," he said shaking his head. His voice wavered off. His face was deeply shaded from his straw hat, turning his eyes into tiny slits.

"Last month it was two men. Down on their knees doing it like dogs do it. In the sunshine. Not a cloud in the sky. This month. Her," he said motioning with a thumb leveled back towards the Catholic section of the cemetery.

"I don't know where the crazies come from. Getting naked out here. But I wish they'd stay home and do it there," he lamented.

The old caretaker walked away from us. Dragging his garbage can with weeds in it after him. Like he was dragging the heaviest burden in the world behind him.

Incident on Caroline

ROBIN ORLANDI

Being so caught up,
So mastered by the brute blood of the air,
Did she put on his knowledge with his power
Before the indifferent beak could let her drop?
WB Yeats

Monica tried to focus on the stars spangled against the van's windshield. The carpet under her back itched. She could still hear the music rocking out from the waterfront where cover bands made tourists forget. Closer, the sound of the men's voices was still there. She felt her eyes closing again. Her eyes were so heavy.

"Our flight leaves at quarter of ten Mona." Rocky waved the tickets. "Can you believe we're going to be wearing shorts in February?" He was ecstatic. The agent had gotten him a great discount on one of the best hotels in Key West, right on Duval Street. His overtime hours covered the cost of the entire trip, and then the boss had thrown in a surprise bonus. And they were going together, their first real vacation in years. And maybe the first one they'd actually remember. Eighteen months sober and counting. Finally the bad parts seemed to be going away.

"Key West isn't the end of the world, but you can see it from here."

"'No sniveling,' I love that." Capt. Easy toasted the sign above the bar and drained his Rolling Rock in one cold swallow. The happy hour crew of sailors and dock dogs around him clinked their glasses in agreement.

"Yeah, gotta take it like a man," said a shrimper in from the Carolinas.

"And bend over," added Billy Kilroy.

"Kilroy, you fuck, you are one preverted dude, everyone from Ohio like you?"

Billy looked up, his milk blue eyes full of deep ocean, a reflection of a squalid sea.

"Nope. Left there. Everybody here though, is..." He thumped the drum at his side, "'bada bom!,' One way or the other."

Easy laughed, "Man, if you are the answer, what was the question?"

Trudy the bartender appeared, nipples leading, their salute thru a thin t-shirt intended for business purposes only. Ditto her red lipstick mouth. Tanned and solid, she carried a ten mug round, "I have the answer Gentlemen, sometimes it's better not to ask."

Billy nodded, "Why we're all here, ain't it?"

"This is a great room baby, look how far down Duval we can see!"

Rocky grinned at Mona's squeaky happy voice. "Up above the world now, told you this time would come."

She flipped a stack of magazines and brochures she'd gathered in the lobby down on the bed. "Ohmigod, look at all the stuff there is to do, we could spend a month at least and not get through all of it."

"Um, and that doesn't include what's not in the brochures, does it?" Rocky pulled her against him, kissing her face, "we can be ourselves here, whatever we want for two weeks."

She smiled at him, "Let's get started you, I can't wait."

They fell into the perpetual stream of locals and visitors flowing up and down Duval Street and made the mandatory crawl from one end to the other to set their compasses to the Rock. They ate conch fritters at the Kraals, planned a trip to the Tortugas, wandered through the city cemetery, scoped the drag queen lineup at the 801 and diligently bypassed bar after bar, ignoring the clinging scent of alcohol lingering in the doorways. He saw her look in, look away, walk on. His mind ran ahead planning, item by item. Charting their course. "Happy Hour Special, Live Blues" said the chalkboard at the corner.

The days ran quickly together. Mona and Rocky worked hard to discard their tourist image. Their tans darkened from long walks on the beach. They found the AIDS Memorial tucked away at the foot of a pier where entire families set up at sunset to dip lines for yellowtail and grunt. They met the Cookie Woman, Marrying Sandy and Horacio, who had been born in Havana and came to Key West on one of the last legal ferry trips.

"Used to be Mallory dock, eh, where we went fishing this time of day, but now you cain't even find the dock there for the people. Now where are you all from did you say?"

Rocky was an avid river fisherman back home and so their conversation filled with fish tales, both salted and fresh. Horacio's little granddaughter took to Mona and when she and Rocky started to leave, the girl trailed them, "Why don't you stay?" Her eyes, like liquid pools of onyx, widened imploringly.

"Don't worry Niña." Mona had learned the endearment from Horacio. "We'll come back to see you." Mona took the sailor's button she'd found on the beach and pressed it into the little girl's hand, "Here, make a wish little doll." That was something else they'd learned, that the fat, smooth, two-tone buttons tangled in seaweed along the water's edge were really seed pods, believed to bring protection and good fortune to their bearers.

"Maybe she's right Rocky."

"What's that Hon?" he asked.

"Maybe she's right," Mona repeated, "maybe we should stay. This place is so easy and relaxed. Wouldn't you like to always be warm and swim everyday?"

He smiled at her. "That would be nice."

On Mallory Square the sun was falling while tourists watched a strong man lift a shopping cart full of cinderblocks with his teeth. House cats walked across a tightrope and a dreadlocked yogin tied himself into a human half hitch. A dozen flavors of music flowed along the dock, but one beat persisted behind all the others, heavy and insistent.

A woman and her pale daughters trailed down the pier, staring at everything like three Dorothies in Oz.

"Mom, what is that?"

"What's what sweetie?"

"That man who's drumming, what's he carrying?" The girls' mother turned to look.

"I don't see what you mean." She scrutinized the bearded man in cutoffs with a fisherman's tan and hands that moved restlessly across the drumhead. Then she saw it move on his shoulder, one clawed foot and a long tail. "Oh!" She shuddered momentarily, "for heavens sake, its some kind of creature, a snake? No, it has legs..."

Her daughters walked toward the man, "Wait, I know mom, that's one of those lizards like on that TV show, what do you call it . . ."

"An inguana" said the second daughter as they approached the reptile.

"Iguana, stupid," her sister corrected.

"Girls . . ." Before the mother could finish Billy had turned toward them, his eyes void as the open sea.

"Well hello ladies." He smiled and they stopped. The lizard flicked its tongue, tasting the late afternoon heat rising off the parking lot. "Let me guess, are you from the midwest? That's my home." He saw the girls staring with fascination at the iguana and lifted it off his shoulder. "Here, don't be scared, he's a love, might hurt a fly but certainly not two pretty young ladies." The girls giggled nervously but held out tentative hands to stroke the cool, lime green hide. "Not to worry mom, he's completely tamed, picked him up during a tour of Southeast Asia." Billy smiled at her disarmingly, blue eyes flashing. "So is this your first trip to our island Ma'am?"

The mother's look of apprehension receded. "Why yes, and I must say, we've never seen anything quite like this before."

He smiled. "No, there's only one Cayo Hueso. After Ohio, this place was some kind of hallucination," he paused, then quickly added, "you know, like a dream, except when you wake up you realize that it's real, and it's such a pleasant relief."

"A relief? Well, I suppose. Did you say Ohio? My sister lives there. We're from Minnesota."

Billy thought to himself, it always shows. He extended the lizard even closer to the girls, "Here, you can hold him, just don't squeeze." They hesitated.

"Go ahead and I'll play a song. Do you like Caribbean music?"

The mother nodded at the girls, "It's OK, if you want to, just be careful. Oh yes, we heard the steel drum band at our hotel last night. They were wonderful."

The oldest stretched out her arm and the lizard crawled onto it, coming to rest on her shoulder. "Eeehhhhww," the girl exhaled.

"It's OK, I'm watching him, it's OK," said her sister.

Billy began stroking the drum. The rhythm built quickly, sinuous and hypnotic. The percussion fixed them in place. The mother coughed reflexively, as if pressed by a foreign hand. It would be impolite to leave in the middle of the song, yet the desire to do so grew suddenly strong in her mind. The lizard crawled from one girl's shoulder onto her sister's.

"Irene?" The deep voice reached through the drumbeat.

"Oh daddy, look at what we found!" The girls turned to display the reptile to their father.

"For the love of mike, what the heck is that thing?" he said sharply.

The beat, risen to a crescendo around them, halted abruptly as the man's voice cut into Billy's consciousness. The father was with them. The flow ended.

"Harold, there you are, this man was playing some Caribbean song for the girls." The quick arch of her eyebrows caught his eye. Like a shiver.

"Well, that's very nice. But our reservation's at eight, so we have to get going now. Girls . . ." He looked at his wife quizzically.

Billy extended his hand to the father, "Nice family you have here."

The father looked at him. "Uh, you betcha, thanks. I don't think my daughters ever saw anything like your animal there before."

"That was awesome," the girls said in unison, and handed the iguana back. "Thanks!"

"Don't mention it," said Billy, smiling straight through them.

"By the way," said the mother, "what was the name of that unusual music you played?" She glanced at her husband.

"That?" he looked down, then directly at her, "It's Haitian," he said, "a Haitian march."

Rocky and Mona started the night on a high note. He'd found a Queen Conch shell at the beach that afternoon, empty but intact. At lunch they were the final table of the day and the waiter had given them the last piece of Key lime pie, and a two coffees, no charge. Back in their room the conch glistened on their bureau like a captive sunset. And at Mallory, watching the real sun drop into the sea, Mona swore she saw the green flash. People tried for years to spot the elusive emerald flash just as the sun slid below the horizon, and it had come to her without effort.

As they were leaving they passed a drum circle, men and women chanting, hands flying in an elaborate quilt of rhythms exotic to both of them.

"Now that's hot. Not even the lot at a Dead concert ever sounded that good, did it Rock?"

The players were covered in sweat, feet moving, bodies arched over hoops of wood and hide, like a heart. Rocky shook his head. "No. Not nearly that complicated. This reminds me of Morocco, of something ancient, like those drummers who played with the Stones."

They stood and listened. From behind them a separate thread of sound entered, fast and raw. The other musicians looked up as the sound floated near, over and into their jam. Three men stopped at the circle, the foreign drum dropping to a single cadence.

"Party's going back over to the Mascot tonight. You hippies can stand here till the cops chase you out or beat feet with us; the *Guadalupe* just got back to port full up and those boys will be buying."

Mona turned to Rocky. "If they leave, let's go over with them, can we? I want to hear what happens."

"Well, I dunno, maybe later Hon, I think we should go eat now, remember Horatio told us we had to try the crawfish enchilada at La Carreta, remember, to ask for it special?"

She pursed her lips. "Yes, but we might not have a chance to hear them all again, I mean some of these musicians are probably just traveling thru, com'on, let's be spontaneous."

He felt an involuntary twinge. Spontaneous had always gotten out of hand. "I bet they'll just be getting started by the time we finish dinner. We've got the whole night ahead, and I know you must be hungry. Afterwards we'll go over, ok?"

For the first time since they'd left, she felt the nick of annoyance, but stopped herself. Don't overreact, first rule. She took a deep breath. "I guess, but we could probably eat at the Mascot too."

Rocky shook his head. He knew wherever the Mascot was, it was a bar, not a restaurant. But pointing that out would be like shining a spotlight. He feinted, "Yeah, but if they don't serve food, we'll starve. Tonight's for enchiladas baby, the Mascot can wait a little bit, let's go on."

She looked at him and mouthed, "OK," turning as she did to look toward the string of musicians slowly departing. The one who had spoken turned suddenly and stared back at them. "Everybody's invited," he said.

Dinner took a long time. The waitress moved slowly and they had to repeat every request, with mixed results. The staccato patter of Cuban Spanish peppered the room. The food that did arrive was excellent, not spicy the way they'd expected, but rich. "Now where did she go to?" Rocky rolled his eyes at Mona, "I guess familiar faces get priority here, sheesh, are they out back slaughtering the pig or what?"

"Take it easy, I'll get her attention when she comes out." Mona watched the kitchen door. "There she is," The waitress had emerged carrying a pitcher filled with fruit floating in a magenta liquid. "Oh, that looks good. Señora?"

The waitress looked at them and held a finger in the air, "Moment." Ten minutes later she returned. "Yes?"

Rocky began to speak but Mona cut in, "The last thing you carried out, what was it, in the pitcher?"

"Ah, Sangria. You want?"

"Now wait a minute Mona."

"Oh come on baby, just one glass, we're going to be here forever and we've been so good, the trip's been great, let's celebrate just a little. It looks so delicious." She widened her eyes at him in a way he knew would be impossible to resist.

"I don't think it's a smart idea, but OK, but just one, agreed?"

Mona nodded and the waitress turned to leave. Rocky didn't hesitate this time, "Excuse me ma'am?"

"Yes?"

"When will our food be ready ?"

"Very busy tonight. Soon, OK?" she said over her shoulder. A few minutes later a busboy appeared with a pitcher of Sangria.

"Oh, wait, we only wanted a glass."

The boy frowned. "She told me bring this here, yes?"

"No," Rocky said. "Just a glass."

"I get her," the boy replied, leaving the pitcher and retreating into the kitchen.

Mona took Rocky's hand, "It's OK, relax, I'll behave. Just for vacation, for now, then no more, I promise." As she spoke she picked up the plastic glass and poured.

Rocky sighed and glanced down at the copy of the Key West Citizen in his lap. The classifieds. Full of low paying jobs and expensive rents. Suddenly he felt discouraged.

"Private excursions. Charter your Mile High Club adventure today!" said an ad.

Walking back from the restaurant, Rocky knew they'd made a mistake.

"Whew, I feel great, I'd forgotten how nice this feels, now that I can handle it, we can really start to have some fun, huh, what's wrong, where's my smile?"

"Mona, I think we should head back to the room now, I feel kinda tired and we've had a long day. Remember, tomorrow we're going out to the Tortugas, we need to be rested up so we can really enjoy it." He smiled weakly.

"Huh? Oh, not yet! The night's young! We have to hear the drummers, you promised."

They parried back and forth, neither making the desired progress. Not paying attention to where they were until a sign caught Mona's eye, "Rocky look, it's 'Adam's Eve,' Adam and Eve, get it?" The overhead sign swayed in the night air. A man and woman wearing only vines were carved into each end of the sign. "Oh," she said, "it's naked."

"What is?"

"This bar is, and it's on the roof too."

"Mona, what in hell are you talking about?" Rocky felt himself slip and regretted it instantly.

"That, Mr. Know It All." She pointed with one hand to a smaller sign that read, "Clothing Optional Rooftop." "I want to see that, and while I'm at it, I think I'd like to have another drink." The defiance in her voice was unmistakable to Rocky.

"Mona, please, you don't need another drink, we were doing fine without the booze. Remember what happens, let's not, OK?"

"No, I *am* doing fine. You think you have to control me, well you don't. I can handle it now." She headed up the stairs.

"Mona!" He looked up at her, wondering how everything had changed so fast.

"Come with me then, you know you want to."

They went upstairs together and drank. Bodies naked and clothed brushed past them at the bar, both men and women. They tried not to stare at first, then realized that everyone was looking, drinking, talking watching. Relaxed.

"Best way to beat the heat," said a tall muscular, man who walked over to order drinks.

"And to meet new friends," giggled the woman with him. Neither wore a stitch. Mona watched them. "They're so free."

"Maybe," said Rocky.

"No, they really are, look at her." Across the bar the woman had started dancing in a slow reggae rhythm, hips and arms swaying. Her husband stood close behind her, smiling and watching her, and the circle of men and women enjoying her motions.

"She's so free and he's protecting her. I wish I could know what that feels like."

"No way are you going to do that Mona, no way." The edge in his voice irritated her.

"God, can't I do anything?"

Rocky didn't answer.

Mona looked back across the bar toward the dancer again and noticed a man who looked familiar. A fisherman, or from the hotel? Then she remembered, the drum circle on the dock.

"Hey, we were going to that place to see drummers again, remember, huh?"

"Nah, its too late for that. Just too late."

"No it's not. There's one, look, he sees us, he'll know." She waved at him.

Billy couldn't figure out who the chick across the bar waving at him was, but she and her old man were sure enough lit up. The band at the Mascot? Oh yeah, they were still there. On their hands and knees and out of their minds. A par-tay.

"It was rocking just a while ago. I'm headed back, why don't you come on over with me?" Billy offered, measuring their reactions.

"Nah, time to go home." Rocky slurred the words.

"Ah, no it's not, I wanna hear those damned drums, why d'you keep tryin' to stop me?"

"Whatever Mona, always have it your way."

Billy said, "Look dude, tell you what, this is where the bar is." He handed Rocky a matchbook. "She ain't gonna give you any peace till she hears them drums, so lets go on over, then you just call a cab to come pick you up there and both of you'll be home in an hour."

Rocky couldn't keep his focus on the man, but cab and home sounded good. "OK, I guess so, let's go."

Halfway through the walk over Rocky spotted a cab and flagged it. "Thas it. Time to go now, Mona." She stood off to the side near Billy, they had been talking about Butch Trucks and John Bonham.

Billy whispered, "It's OK if you want to stay on, I'll make sure you get back later. Someone will give you a ride."

Something smelled sweet in the night air. The tropics. Drums. Another drink. "Ain't going Rock, I'm going to hear the music, then I'll be back. Not long."

"I'm not asking again Mona, come on."

"Screw you, get a life, I told you, I'll be there, when the music's over."

"You're wasted Mona, nothin's changed."

The cabbie grumbled, "Hurry up man, I don't have all night."

Rocky climbed in and held the door open,

"You coming or not?"

"No, go away." She ran to catch up to the drummer, who'd kept slowly walking.

What were they talking about? She could barely hear him. The lights throbbed around Mona in the dark bar, the drumbeat pounded and invaded her, nothing was in the way. Not work, not Rocky, not twelve steps, she was a freebird, like in the song. She'd lost track of who was playing, of the shots he'd bought, of the time.

"So you liked seeing that woman dance at Adam's huh?" he asked.

"Um, she was so uninhibited, so open to everything."

"You're like that too, you know, you've been dancing since we got here."

Mona swayed and giggled, "Have I?" she focused hard on him; his look seemed strange, then it was gone. She paused, then another voice came "Hey Billy, who's the new lady? Another round over here. How about a little toot?"

She snorted hard on the bullet, picked up the new beer and said suddenly, "So how do you know so much?"

Billy's fingers closed around her wrist, " About being so-called free? I know cause I grew up on my own, with no people, and flophouse rules. On the street you beat or get beaten, simple. My Uncle Sam showed me the rest and since then, I do what I want. Bang my drum. You like that idea, don't you?"

She paused, "Sounds hard. But you can be like an animal then, spontaneous."

He looked hungrily at her, "Does that make you wet?" She felt his hand move against the inside of her thigh.

"Oh, you shouldn't do that."

"I thought you were free."

She headed out to dance and he followed. Soon after, his mouth met hers.

"You're like a piece of candy, you know that?" he said.

She could barely hear the music over his labored breathing. She remembered trying not to, being too drunk to stop him, and then screaming at the edges of pleasure she didn't remember. Her body ached in new places, slippery. So tired. Where was she? He was over her and she didn't recognize the expression on his face at all. "You like it all don't you, just a dirty little whore."

She frowned. "Don't say that, we're having fun's all."

He sat back and tapped the drum by the couch, "Oh yeah, big fun in Paradise. Tell it on Duval Street. This is my song, the Ton Ton Macoute play it in Haiti." She looked at the wall behind him that would not hold still. His face melted like a watercolor. He stopped.

"Let me see how much fun you want to have."

She felt him slide something between her legs again, maybe good, then suddenly not good, "No, not so deep, take it easy." She pushed him back.

"But you wanted wild didn't you baby, you sore, aww, then let's try the backdoor." In one motion Billy slipped the toy in. She moaned.

"You like that huh?"

Mona shook her head no, the words barely forming, "It hurts, don't!" and tried to sit up.

He shoved her down, "Oh no, I want you to take it, you wanted it." She tried to shove him away, but he rammed into her faster and faster, frenzied watching her writhe, unable to stop.

"Easy man, you got to help me." Capt. Easy looked up at Billy and stepped back, "Shit , what happened to you?" Sweat was pouring off of Billy, over a patchwork of scratches running down his bare chest, his hair soaked and tangled.

"Man, I don't know, I was screwing this crazy, drunk chick and she started freaking and passed out in my living room, she's having some kinda fit."

"Jesus Christ Bill, is there any trouble you don't get into?" A few of the other men remaining in the bar gathered around them. "He's gone and fucked some girl half to death apparently," Easy reported.

"No man, it's worse than that, I gotta get her out of there. I need somebody with a car." Billy fidgeted trying to light a cigarette.

The men all looked at him. Tiny Pete and one of the *Guadalupe* fishermen shook their heads and turned away, "Too rich for our blood man, got enough troubles as it is."

"I'll go, my van's out back, it sounds like she's in trouble; you're a fuckin' nutcase Bill, always on with that Haitian Death March crap and now this." Easy turned to his massive friend. "Hey Ramon, thanks man, let's try to stay cool eh, can't help anybody elsewise."

The last thing Mona saw was the North Star dancing its steady course far away, behind the cracked glass of Ramon's windshield. A day later, she was front-page news.

Billy fled and was captured in Reno, returned to Key West and convicted of first-degree murder. The trial's lurid headlines dismayed even the most trade-hardened locals. Some line in the heated sands of Paradise had been crossed and no one could get comfortable with the result. Play was supposed to forgive. Death didn't. How the two got so mixed up was anyone's guess. The lights had been turned up way high at the end of the party, and it looked awful.

Drums play on in Cayo Hueso, for reasons both sacred and profane. The Mascot's long gone and the commercial boats work out of Stock Island now. But you can still find Adam's Eve on Duval Street, and take a trip upstairs to strip your innocence, if you dare.

Feathered Friends

THERESA FOLEY

The odor of death was coming up from under the house for three weeks before she found the first body. Maggie lived in a small Conch cottage built 70 years ago on a narrow Key West street in the Cuban part of town. It was not the historic gentrified neighborhood of million dollar sea captains' mansions, all gingerbread-trimmed with perfect Traveler's Palms in their gardens and full of winter folks and wealthy gay couples. No, Maggie resided in a small white house with pink and green trim on a block with no sidewalks where the neighbors spent 14 hours each day sitting on their front stoops drinking beer and speaking in Spanish to each other, as if they'd fallen out of synch with the times years before and really didn't care.

She was the outsider here with her pale skin, living alone in a house with six rooms, with all her Cuban-American neighbors, who'd been there far longer than she, packing in a half dozen family members into smaller houses. They treated her courteously even if she didn't understand more than a few words of the Spanish that flew around the street each day like the warblers that came in springtime.

The one exception was her neighbor right next door, an odd and offensive little man who kept his house and yard meticulous, but smelled like a barnyard. Maggie had been downwind of him enough times when he'd corner her on the street and tried to carry on long conversations about things like what he fed his cats to know certain things about him. His name was Guiseppe, and he came from Europe, not Cuba.

Before Maggie bought the little house, they'd warned her about the roosters. She'd been there a month when the babies arrived.

"Noise bother you?" asked Wanda, her friend who'd lived in the house before her. "They're gonna wake you up every night until you get used to it. These are city roosters. They don't know dawn from a streetlamp."

The brilliantly plumed birds roamed free all over the neighborhood. Crowing at the top of their lungs anytime of day or night, fierce, merciless and comical.

The crowing bothered some people but Maggie just bought herself a big box of foam earplugs. Before long she actually started enjoying the racket. The roosters with their testosterone charged antics reminded her of some of the men she knew. First there was the way they relentlessly chased the hens, a nonstop occupation. A couple of times a day, a rooster would jump a hen, usually out in the front yard or the street in front of the tourists who parked there to go to the Cuban restaurant at the corner. The squawking sounded like the hen was being murdered, but it only lasted about a minute and then the rooster would hop off and behave in a dignified aloof way again, just like some of the men she knew. The funniest thing the roosters would do was to flap their multi-colored wings hard enough to launch themselves six or eight feet into the air, on top of some elevated platform like her fence. Once on his podium, the rooster would let out a crowing, chest-puffing display of noise, telling the world that this rooster knew it all and you damn well better give him your attention. Yes, a rooster was like a man.

Maggie was a painter and she worked in a small studio at the back of the house. The studio's glass doors opened onto the garden, where the mama hens loved to roost and feed. It was quiet and protected, and perfect for having babies. By spring, four or five chicken families had taken up residence. Maggie watched them until she could tell each family apart, each mother having slightly different coloring, or a tuft of feathers in a novel place. She fed them birdseed in the morning and tried to protect them from the stray cats. She fell into the habit of counting the babies when they weren't hiding under their mothers.

When a mama hen first hatched her brood, there'd be seven or nine or even sometimes 11 of the tiny balls of feathers. The bigger the brood, the more likely that two or three would be small and weak, looking like little nuclear war survivors, staggering around with scrawny wings and more skin than fluff. Those were the ones she wanted to save the most, and the ones she could do nothing for. Each morning while the babies were tiny, she would count one less in each family. The hens could only protect perhaps three little chicks and as the numbers dwindled, the grim realization set in that as she slept safe in her bed at night baby chickens crossed to the other side right underneath her.

Once a chick got to be about six inches tall, it became a hardy and self-sufficient creature. There'd been a bumper crop of chickens that spring when she got the house. One morning she counted 40 chickens and six roosters right in her yard. Her friends thought the chickens were excessive and taking over in an unhealthy way but Maggie loved having them around, wondering if she had become chicken-obsessed because she never lived on a farm as a child.

She was just getting out her paint brushes, the day she noticed the strong smell the first time. She sniffed and decided to light some incense, assuming it was just one of those fleeting moldy tropic smells that come and go in all Key West houses. But it didn't go away after two days, and as the overpowering stench of decay followed her from room to room, she knew it wasn't going to go away until she did something about it.

Outside, she searched the yard. She looked beneath the areca palms, and behind the ferns and hibiscus bushes. Nothing. Behind the pool equipment. Nothing. Then under the house, which was elevated about 18 inches off the ground and rested on cinder blocks in classic Conch style.

There, about a foot beyond the edge was a large clump of feathers, arranged as if they'd been melted and set in wax. Black flies circled the unidentifiable lump. She coughed and backed away but the smell had already sunk deep into her chest. There was nothing else to do but get a shovel and black plastic bag, and hold her breath as she scooped the pile up. She looked up at the sky and asked spirit to take the chicken. It fell into pieces, but she managed to get it all, and prayed a little for her deceased chicken friend. The corpse went unceremoniously into the garbage can.

Still the odor lingered inside the house. It took ten minutes of searching between the palms and bananas to find the second soft pile of feathers and bones. Over the next few days, Maggie went out again and again, that distinctive smell of death chasing her out of her peaceful, little rooms in search of yet another body. After five days and 11 dead chickens, she'd had just about enough.

She'd always been the kind of person who couldn't keep quiet when she saw something unjust or inhumane. Who to call? The Wildlife Rescue people might help, after all, the chickens were wild all over the island.

"No, there is no disease killing chickens on the island that I'm aware of," said the lady who answered her call. "Sounds like somebody's poisoning them. There's not much I can do but if you can get a body that's only been dead an hour or less, I may be able to have it tested and tell you what it died from. Call me back if you have any other questions."

Maggie called the Key West Police Department. An hour later, a hefty young policeman knocked on the door. When she told him the problem, he didn't even bother to pull out his notepad.

"Unless YOU can prove it's poisoning, there's nothing I can do," he said.

"Are you trying to tell me you won't even file a report?"

"If you provide me with findings of poisoning, then I could write an animal cruelty report," he said.

"And then what?"

He shrugged and headed back to his air-conditioned cruiser. So 15 dead birds didn't constitute a crime. Not only did the Key West Police Department expect her to prove that something illegal had occurred, they also wanted her to investigate who'd done it. She lived in a town with the highest tax rate in the whole state, almost no crime and a police department that expected the citizens to do their work for them.

Who to call next, when vigilante justice seemed to be the only option? The fourth estate. The newspaper was supposed to afflict the comfortable and comfort the afflicted, wasn't it? Maggie dialed the number for the Citizen and asked for the newsroom. The editor listened to her.

"Sounds like a story, but I can't promise anything," she said.

An hour later, a photographer was out in front of the house, snapping photos of her and one of the remaining wild roosters, a large, brilliant bird with feathers that shimmered purple in the sunlight.

Meanwhile, more odors, more bodies. She shoveled the remains of a large beautiful rooster that fell apart in chunks into a bag. A hen had just expired and its body held together sufficiently to be transported out to Stock Island, to a vet's office, where the Wildlife Rescue lady had directed her to bring a carcass in for poison testing. "It has to be fresh," she said. This one might do; at least it wasn't falling off its bones.

When she got home, the phone was ringing. It was Wanda.

"Someone is poisoning my chickens, and I think I know who," Maggie said.

"Poison? Who would do such a thing?"

"I think I know."

"Nobody would poison the chickens."

"My neighbor might. He hates them." The recluse who didn't know the meaning of the word soap made no secret of his contempt for those sweet, downy-feathered creatures. He ordered Maggie several times to stop feeding them. He told her friends who lived down the block, "She feeds them! She feeds them!"

One day she came out on the front porch to check for the mail and Guiseppe came flying through the shrubbery right into her yard wielding a broom, looking like a crazed rooster himself. He was in pursuit of one of the smaller, faster males, apparently intent on whacking it to death to silence the incessant cockadoodle-doing. She stared at him and he finally raised his eyes toward the house and saw that he was being watched. "They are driving me crazy!" he yelled, retreating back towards his own house, broomstick in hand.

But the most blatant sign was Guiseppe's habit, each day at approximately 5 a.m., of screaming at the top of his lungs, "Die chickens, die. Die! Die! Die!"

Her house was only 15 feet from his window, another charming Key West architectural feature, and the war cry woke her every morning before dawn. The roosters interpreted his protests as appreciation, and only crowed more enthusiastically in response. Maybe they knew he was a chicken hater, and being small birds, realized that crowing was their only means of counterforce. She'd pull a pillow over her head and go to sleep for 45 minutes until the first semi tractor-trailer trucks arrived an hour before dawn arrived to begin unloading crates of frozen food to the Cuban restaurant across the street.

The trucks and their crews were only about 1,000 times noisier than the roosters. Spanish-speaking teamsters would begin to throw dozens of boxes of frozen, processed food — pork, fish and fries — that would later be transformed into Cuban cuisine — from the eight-foot-high truck bed onto the street, making a constant slap-slap-slapping that resonated through the little wooden houses on their cinderblock stilts. The vibrations alone would wake a person. The racket would go on for about an hour, punctuated by the noise of a loose-wheeled, overloaded delivery cart rattling its way to the restaurant door. Maggie went outside in her pajamas to ask the men to quiet down or wait until a decent hour to start their delivery, but they only laughed at her in Spanish. She called the restaurant manager to complain and he hung up on her.

She told Wanda, "I don't know why my neighbor doesn't scream at the trucks instead of the roosters. They are ten times worse."

"The truckers would come over and kick his ass. The roosters aren't going to fight back," Wanda answered.

Maggie decided to write a letter to everyone on the block, pleading for the chickens' lives and asking that the poison be taken up. In it, she made the case that poison wasn't good for children or cats, hoping that the perpetrator had some sense of logic and decency. She stuck the letter in the mailbox of each house and taped it to the light poles on the street.

She slept fitfully that night, wondering how many chickens were twitching and taking their last tiny breaths underneath the house as she slept. Early the next morning, Maggie wandered across the street to the metal boxes that sold newspapers in front of the Cuban restaurant. She put in her fifty cents for a Citizen, and saw her photo on page 1 at the very top, under the headline, "Foul Play Suspected in Chicken Disappearances."

Things really started to happen then. She'd been painting an hour when the wildlife lady called and told her there was a New York City TV crew in town, wanting to do a story on chickens. She wanted to give them Maggie's number.

If it would save the life of even one chicken, Maggie was willing to do it, so she said yes. An hour later, a reporter, producer, cameraman and soundman from Comedy Central's Daily News program were knocking at her door.

"We'd been planning on reporting on the overpopulation problem down here," said Alexis, the pretty blond producer, who looked like she was still in college. "Too many chickens born this year. But this, a serial murderer of chickens, well, this is more interesting."

Maggie realized that the assignment was probably more related to the desire to get out of New York and close to the beach for a few days than anything else.

The crew set up in Maggie's garden and stayed for three hours, videotaping her for practically the entire time. Two hours of interviewing for three minutes of airtime.

The first few questions from the reporter, Rollo Pink, were fine. Rollo moved smoothly through his routine with his wide brown eyes and an expensive haircut that marked him as an out of towner. He was definitely not innocent looking but had a certain kind of New York slickness about him.

Rollo began to fire off questions: "Do you have any idea who might have killed these chickens?"

"What should the police be looking for in profiling this killer?"

"Have you seen any suspicious characters lurking about your yard?

And, forgive me for asking this, but is it possible that you might be a chicken hater yourself?"

Rollo was sweating profusely in his three-piece vanilla linen suit in the humid 90-degree Florida afternoon.

Then he accused her of having murdered the chickens. "Does it seem strange that the chickens didn't start dying till you moved to the island? A coinkidink?" he asked, batting his eyelids at her.

The effect the TV camera had on her was to flip her into a trance-like state in which she was as childlike and obedient as Rollo was obnoxious and crude. Her usual outspoken demeanor had been replaced by a polite, frozen desire to be helpful. At one point Maggie wanted to yell at him, "Grow up!" but she didn't.

He began to ask about the roosters, how aggressive they were, how bothersome. In the first few questions, he used the word rooster. Then Rollo adlibbed: "What does one do when you have a big cock running rampant in your yard?"

At the word cock, Alexis, Maggie and the rest of the crew smirked and snickered. Rollo's eyes lit up, and he was off like a thoroughbred out of the Kentucky Derby gates.

"How does one catch a big cock?"

"When you use gloves to handle a cock, what kind of gloves are they, are they rough?"

"Is a Key West cock meaner than a New York City cock?" and so on, and on, over and over.

Maggie stayed in her chair, answering the questions with a straight face, and only occasionally admonishing him, "It's nothing like what you think. You are acting a bit childish here, Rollo."

Sitting there with a frozen grin on her face, trying to be polite, answer his questions, while in the back of her mind, mental klaxons screamed their alarm. He's totally making fun of the whole sad situation. He's turning the dead chickens into some kind of sick rooster sex joke. She asked herself, why are you going along with this?

Alexis sat in the corner, giggling and saying, "We need to shoot that one over" whenever Rollo flubbed one of his lines. Each question was repeated three or four times to get Rollo from several different angles, as if getting his profile just right was going to make or break this piece of television journalism.

Everyone was laughing now at all the crude comments, and Maggie had to admit, his immature display appealed to some demented aspect of her own personality. To finish up, they went out front and they taped her scooping up a fresh carcass into a black plastic bag. The remains fell off the bones for the camera as she lifted the shovel full of her former feathered friend. Once they packed up the cameras and left her alone, reality sunk in: The chance was remarkably high that she would end up looking pretty stupid when the show aired on national television. Her only excuse would be, "Well, I do live in Key West."

They hadn't been gone long with the kid across the street, Armando, was knocking on her door. Armando lived with his mother and grandfather, a older Cuban gentlemen whose English seemed to be limited to the "Hello baby," that he called out to Maggie from his easy chair on their front porch. Armando would translate for his grandfather the few times she went over to talk to them.

On the day she posted the neighborhood letter, Armando had told her, "We've picked up 15 dead chickens here."

They were in the pro-chicken camp. Armando told her, "My grandfather wants to build a huge chicken coop out back so no more chickens would be poisoned."

"Two chickens just died in our yard," he said. "The paper said you needed a fresh one."

Maggie sighed. She didn't have the energy to deal with another drive out to the veterinarian's office. Early that morning, the vet called to say the first two bodies had been too old to yield results. But she had to do what she could, so she told Armando to put the bodies into a bag and bring them to her.

He carried them across the street in a single plastic grocery store sack, and handed it to her. The bag flopped and shook.

"One of them is still alive," he said.

She took the bag to her car and drove it out for the tests, then came home, exhausted.

Later that night, the house was quiet, the excitement of having the camera crew around had died, and all she could think was that she'd let the chickens down. She thought of the war in Kosovo and the mass graves being uncovered, and how the stench must be about a million times stronger than her backyard odors. Her chicken war seemed pretty trivial in comparison but it was hitting her just as hard. She was just too sensitive, or maybe it was that everybody else was not sensitive enough. A few days later, Comedy Central aired their Key West chicken story, and the whole country had its chance to laugh at the dead chicken story.

She went away on a trip one day, returned a week later, and all the sex-crazed roosters and their patient little hens and babies had disappeared, like peasants in a Latin American dictatorship. All the chickens were gone, save for one lonely hen that would run up and down the middle of the street.

"What happened to the chickens?" she asked Armando.

"Somebody came in a van and trapped them all and took them away," he said. Armando pointed to Guiseppe's clean white house with the pink bougainvillea in the yard. "He got a lady to come and take all the chickens away."

The street didn't feel quite the same after the chicken wars ended. Maggie stopped eating chicken for good then. The last few times she was served chicken on a plane or in a restaurant, she couldn't help but think of their small bodies falling to pieces as she shoveled the carcasses into the garbage bags. And a tiny piece of good news had come about a week after the TV crew left to go back to New York. The wildlife lady called Maggie one morning to tell her, "You know the chicken you brought in that was still alive?"

"Sure."

"Well, they were able to give it something to revive it. Someone who works at the vet's office took it home, and now it's their pet."

Maggie was happy for a moment but she couldn't stop thinking about the others. She knew that vegetarians in India believe that intolerance exists in the world because humans ingest the fear that floods through an animal at its moment of death. It was an extreme idea. She knew her friends whispered that she was crazy and wanted her to stop talking that way, but Maggie didn't know how else to explain the fact that people would get so worked up that they'd begin murdering the wild chickens of Key West.

Chickens are now gone from Maggie's part of Margaret Street, and are disappearing all over the island. The battle zone has moved on. Neighbor against neighbor, husband against wife, animal lover against meat eater, local against snowbird, Key West becomes picture perfect.

Love in the Tropics

CONSTANCE GILBERT

He was rangy still, touched yet by the remaining awkwardness of late adolescence, all limbs and sudden physical adjustments. His elbows were propped on the kitchen table, dinner long over and the dishes cleared, and when he slid his arms down, laying his head with its unruly, fiery curls on the table, his left elbow knocked over the little silvertone vase holding the wilting red hibiscus.

Not much water spilled. The bud vase didn't hold much. Still, she leapt up and grabbed the dingy sponge from the back rim of the sink. In a single swath, the water was removed and she tossed the sponge back into its place.

She righted the waterless vase, replaced the flower to a hastening demise.

She was an aging centerfold with heavy breasts extending with the aggressiveness of sturdy lingerie from a ribcage so small as to appear frail. Hips, too, were generous, making the waist — when visible — seem absurdly small.

This tropical spring night, however, little was visible except the pain around the eyes. She rummaged, in a brain slightly benumbed by betrayal and alcohol, for the right words. The exact expression. The truth. If she could find it, her child might avoid the sins of the fathers, the mothers, the whole culture of smothering and criticism and stereotypes and need.

Identical pairs of eyes caught and held each other in the silence of the cluttered kitchen. If it were not for the eyes, the throwback coloring, I could disown him, she thought. Except for the indelible memory of the moment he was born. The rest is his father, identical and antithetical.

But the coloring was hers, too, a generation removed. What else? Were they souls long connected or a single lifetime's lesson? He was born challenging, she realized. She was startled, then, at the moment of his birth, by the look on his face, a look of challenge, and it had not abated for 15 years. What could she say that would not, from the bottomless well of his rebellious intellect, be rejected? Or at least challenged?

The other two were more of a mix, genetically, and still young, distinctly their boisterous blond selves, but still innocent of the crucible of puberty. Still welcome to spend school vacations like this one in the fancy new house upstate, on open water Gulfside, all glass and cedar and angles and built-in toy boxes and desks for their new computers. They were still beloved by a step-mom who was young and glamorous and docile and barren; therefore, they were still indulged by a middle-aged father besotted with a new wife, a new life, a more elegant lifestyle than the one he had chosen, happily enough, for two decades in the confines of a two by four mile island.

"I have a funny notion of love," she said finally. His bushy red eyebrows rose slightly, but he did not speak.

"An old fashioned notion," she continued. Was it a slight frown she saw? Still, the identical dark almond eyes held firm. She rubbed a hand, suddenly damp, along the thightop of the faded cutoff jeans, pushed up the left sleeve of a worn Fantasy Fest T-shirt, scratched absently, and took a healthy swig from the warming bottle of Kelly's microbrew.

"Not funny ha-ha," she said finally. "Funny peculiar — at least in this world. It has to do with the old 'for better or worse'. Out of date, I know."

She smiled ruefully, crookedly. That smile, whether she knew it or not, was one of her predominant charms.

"You meet someone — someone very special. The head knows, and the heart knows and the crotch knows. In my case," she admitted, "the crotch usually knows first. I guess I'd better work to change that. If it ever happens again."

She smiled.

Still he said nothing, just looked at her out of her own almond eyes.

"It's extraordinary," she said, remembering. "The bolt of lightning. You know there's something remarkable here. Uncle Will was my very first love. He was the most beautiful man I'd ever seen. Dad was — what? An awareness. An inevitability. In the middle of our very first date, right up front by the stage at Schooner Wharf, a separate little gong sounded in my head. A voice — never heard it before, never heard it since — said, 'This is the one. You're going to marry him.' That was it; I was a gone goose.

"Aunt Julia — we were sharing that studio on Thomas Street, about the size of your bedroom — she thought I was nuts. But Dad and I were married six months later." She took another swig of beer.

"So," he said.

"So," she said. "It's something you know, gut level." How could he know at 15? Something inaudible screamed at her.

She tried again. "This is someone so dear, so valuable, that you commit to them. Not instantly. That would be dumb, maybe fatal. But you get to know them, really know them, and you commit to them — forever, as it turns out. Read Erich Fromm. You commit yourself to love them — which only means that you know them and respect them, care about them, are concerned about them, and the erotic is included, but it's not the main thing. It shouldn't be the first thing. But once you commit, it's forever."

The boy laughed.

"It told you it was old fashioned."

"You loved Dad forever?" The challenge was in his eyes, in his spine that stiffened as both hands grasped the edge of the table, shaking the fading hibiscus.

"Yes," she said. "I love your father. I wish the best for him. I wish him happiness."

"After what he's done?"

"After what he's —" she stopped dead, picked up her bottle, saw it was empty. Swiveling in her chair, she opened the fridge and grabbed an identical brown bottle. "Want a soda?" she asked.

He shook his head, impatient. "After what he's done?"

God, she thought. How does one love a creature who can reject his own child? But it was truth time. She honestly did not think of what he might have done to her. He did not beat her. He did not wander off after work, leaving her alone. On the contrary, she wandered off — dashed off — frantic after a day of mothering, to rush out and try to change the world. What he had done, ultimately — and it took 12 years — was to be a typical male.

No big deal, she thought. How did he stay so good — so atypical — so long?

"Poor thing, of course I love him," she said. "Not anywhere near how I love you, of course, and I'm angry about — so much." She stopped again. "But anger doesn't mean you stop loving. If it did, you and the little guys would've been dead meat long ago."

She smiled at him. Was that a small smile coming?

She was on a roll. "Loving's why there's anger. Otherwise you wouldn't give a shit. Anger's hating, and that's just the other side of the coin of loving."

"Jesus," he said. "Are you still seeing that shrink?"

"Yes."

"Maybe I oughtta go again."

"I've asked you. Asked you and asked you." For long moments there was silence. She tipped her head back and drank beer.

"Well, maybe we better," he said.

Suddenly, silently, she began to cry. Tears spilled, then flooded her cheeks. Shocked, she tried to speak, to reassure him, to praise him. But her throat was too constricted; what came out was a huge sob, and her thin shoulders shook.

"Mom." He rose and went to her. "Mom. Oh, Mom," he said.

What By Living Here We Gain

ALLEN MEECE

He abandoned his estranged wife and high tech career in Chicago and took the bus south to work on the shrimp boats.

There had been a death on the subway the day he made the decision to leave. It was a gray winter's day, everyone on the subway was wearing gray coats and had blank faces, no more than ants in a subterranean channel repeating a daily journey to nowhere. The train stopped in the black tunnel and they sat there for half an hour, not looking at each other, not talking to each other, trapped. Later he heard that someone had jumped in front of the train and died.

He found himself wondering what it feels like to have a train bust your skull and roll over you and scissor your body in half against the steel rails and some poor transit employee has to pick up the slippery guts that used to be your responsibility. Can you feel shame after you're dead?

Thinking about suicide means you're thinking about suiciding. It was time to abandon ship. He was sinking.

Oh, he looked good on the outside. He wore a suit, had a company car, a cute wife and daughter and son, a "millionaire's family," his wife called them. They rented a nice townhouse with polished oaken floors and a picture window on a grassy ravine. He bought a sailboat on credit and raced it every other Saturday and won a championship two years in a row. He liked being on the water but summer only lasted three months and then it was back to the winter treadmill of work and debt with ten dollars left after the bills were paid and it went on year after weary year. His wife said he was drinking too much and suggested a trial separation. His retort would have been that they should move to a cheaper place and save some money but he knew she wouldn't change so he moved into a cheap sleeping room that smelled like a latrine because the toilet down the hall overflowed regularly.

Then the department store phoned him at work and informed him that he was way over the limit on his credit card.

"You've made a mistake," he said. "We never use that card, it's just for emergency purchases."

"Your wife regularly makes purchases by telephone and has them delivered to your residence," he was told.

We're not even living together and she's piling debt on me, he thought.

He stopped by the house one day while he was on his route of fruitless sales calls. She had the fan running and the weather was cool. He had told her they had to control the electricity bill and only run the fan when there was a heat wave. That was the condition for purchasing the fan that they couldn't afford in the first place. She was cleaning the oaken floor and he, or something within him, walked up and slapped her.

"You don't scare me, mister," she pluckily responded.

"You're too stupid to be scared," a sickness in him said. He loved her deeply all the time but the lifestyle was a growing insanity. He'd made some bad turns along the way and the path was lost.

One week later he made a deal to drive a retired couple's Oldsmobile south to Tampa so they could relax and ride an airplane to their winter house. It was early February, 1977, and a giant windy blizzard hit the Midwest and closed Interstate 75. He was no stranger to winter driving conditions and thought he could skirt the snowstorm by going around it to the east and then to the west, but Ohio was indeed closed. The National Guard was at the intersections with front-end loaders, moving the snow off the highways but the wind blew it back every twenty minutes. He pulled to the side of the road under a bridge and waited for the wind to die down so the plows could clear the road.

Here's my signal to go back, he thought. Back to what? More of the same. That bed is broken and that door closed. This car is going to Tampa even if it takes all winter.

There were just four shrimp boats home ported in Tampa and the shrimpers said go to Key West if you want to get on a boat, they got hundreds down there. But watch out, Key West is a party town. Luckily, he didn't know that that meant he could become a drunk. At that time in his life he might not have accepted the risk.

He caught the bus and arrived in Key West with one hundred and twenty dollars in his pocket. He spent twenty dollars celebrating at the Half Shell Raw Bar, eating conch fritters and getting drunk and admiring the shrimpers getting drunk. They were hard-working and hard-drinking. They didn't commute to the goddam office, they were alive.

As he went to sleep under casuarinas by the sea, he suddenly, happily, realized that the winter can't kill you here. He had been a zombie that emerged from a cold grave to find that it was springtime outside.

The cops woke him up and accurately judged him to be intoxicated and so put him in jail overnight.

He found a storehouse near the sea that had casuarinas growing beside it which could be shinnied up to the flat roof where he slept for months on his own private "penthouse." He was turned-in by a nervous geek, much as he had once been, and the cops arrested him for trespassing.

He found a large cardboard box laying behind the old Key West Handprint Factory. It was a shipping container for the big bolts of cloth that they screen-printed and made into tourist clothes. He cut a window in it and slept in that for weeks until the factory threw it away.

He finally landed a berth on a shrimp boat but found that the boats which would accept his inexperience contained shrimpers who drank almost as much while on the Gulf of Mexico as they did on land. They made it dangerous to work around the heavy trawling equipment. They didn't catch much shrimp and barely made beer money.

His missed his family and the old delusion of getting somewhere even though he hadn't been. Maybe the island life was another wrong turn. Maybe the other world wasn't much worse than this one. He decided to go north. He stuck his thumb out at the foot of US 1 and the cops arrested him for hitchhiking.

A few days later he made a cardboard sign that said "CHICAGO" and sat beside US 1, this time above the city limits and without sticking his thumb out and the cops left him alone. He found a camaraderie on the road, his rides sympathized with his plight and gave him money and snacks. Four days later he checked into a Christian mission on the edge of Skokie where empty men investigated each other's penises in the bathroom stalls. He called his wife and arranged a meeting which she failed to attend. He went to her apartment block and saw her and his children arriving in an expensive car with a man driving. It was time to fight or flee. A violent emotion pushed him to tear that bastard apart but his brain remained cool enough to admit he was a divorced bad news ghost and he fled.

He didn't go back to the mission but found a sailing catamaran drawn up on the grass beside Lake Michigan and he lay beneath the trampoline. The night was damp and cold. He thought of the way the palm fronds clatter in the sunny breeze from the Gulfstream. The water's like clear jade and full of life and you can swim in it any time of year. Just walk right in and swim for free and it's better than anything they have here. With morons' cars on Chicago's Lakeshore Drive roaring and flashing behind him he knew that being broke in paradise was extremely better than being rich in hell. She had recovered, now it was his turn.

When he arrived in Key West the second time he knew the ropes. You're not gonna make enough to pay rent so find a place to sleep where the diligent paradise police can't find you. Get a bike because the town provides no place to sit and rest. Not having your own room, you're gonna be on your feet all day without a bike. Learn where the water fountains are because cold drinks are a costly commodity. Keep neat and clean so the hotels will think you're a tourist and say nothing when you take a refreshing dip in their pools. It's as cheap to buy clothes at the Salvation Army as it is to wash them at the laundromat. Rinse them in the sea until they won't come clean anymore and then throw them away. Own no more than what can fit into a bicycle basket so you'll be mobile and free of worry about stuff.

He found a spot in the old Salt Ponds where, except for the airport noise, it was naturally quiet and beautiful. He slept on a carpet remnant with his rolled clothes for a pillow and a sheet over his nudity. He had a plastic raincover for the brief tropical showers. He stashed his bedroll under the leaves when he went to work and left no trash at his home site. He worked at The Queen's Table restaurant for the regal rate of six bucks an hour and a free meal. But it only took twenty bucks a week to fulfill his needs. For the first time in Consumer Nation he learned how little, not how much, it took to live well.

One night as he was strolling Duval he saw a group gathered in an art gallery reading poetry to each other. There were bottles of wine on the table and a sign that said it was an open reading and all were welcome. He went in to see if the wine was free.

The poems were mostly about honesty, calling spades spades and saying how the poets felt about the shit that went down everywhere. He was amazed that anyone shared their thoughts in public. He had been of the warrior caste, had lived on military bases much of his life where you had to keep your mouth shut about your feelings. He listened and had some of their wine. He liked the taste. He found what he'd been missing all his life; sharing. He began to write. It only took a pen and paper and time. He had plenty.

He wrote about the man in Che Che's Bar who drank a fifth of brandy every day since his wife died and how the door to his house on Truman Avenue stood open to the street for a year after the brandy killed him.

He wrote poems about how people can change their minds and their morals and forget they're living for pointless self-gratification. He wrote of money making people do things they'd never normally do.

He built the DePoo Hospital on a hot empty lot behind K-Mart and sweated so much he was as soggy as if he had just come out of the ocean. He wrote about the successful contractor who had everything except a sexy blonde in a Corvette, so he went out and got that too. His wife found out and she got his business and now the guy's a plumber living in a Stock Island trailer with a woman you wouldn't show mom.

He even wrote a novel, *The Abel Mutiny,* about how savagely wrong the Viet Nam War had been and how the government and most of the population were cretins.

He had to come back to the island to learn what was hard to see in the land of indoor living — society is as stupid as the majority of its constituents so please yourself. And never pay rent.

He saved and bought a boat and moved onto the water at Boca Chica Bay. The cops arrested him for mooring his boat too close to federal highway number one. Oh well, paradise needs a few hurdles or everyone would come down and ruin it. He moved the "Mangrover" a hundred feet from shore and was left alone.

He swam from his eighteen-foot private yacht every day and felt the saltwater soak the angry tension out of him like a ground wire does to a lightning rod. The Gulfstream replaced stingy competitive materialism with the mellow vibrations of the real world. Sunlight entered his soul and chased the dollar signs away.

That's what by living here he gained.

BAITS

BOB MAYO

When we lived inland and fished creeks, rivers and ponds, my friend Mike and I usually sank our vessel on the first day of the fishing season. We did not plan these events. The sinkings were accidental. There was always a good deal of laughter.

The water was never over our heads, there were no giant waves and we were much larger than the fish in the ponds. A safe thing. Then Mike went to heaven and I came home to Key West where I belong. So we stopped sinking together, and for a while I really missed it.

My wife and I needed help dealing hot dogs out a window onto Duval Street from beside a famous bar. The Frenchman came in thin and eager, too white for here and dressed like Europe, grabbed a bun and became our friend. Worked possessed, honest and fair, looked you in the eye like he should and with those qualities, drew to himself a woman to share his life from the crowd that swam by.

Tall blue-eyed country girl from near Germany in his homeland, spoke four languages, and his. She went to work for us too. Throw in a girl from Hong Kong who insisted that I was pretty much right about everything (I loved her), and that there was in fact a Tara, near Atlanta, which would be her next stop. Being a native Georgian, I never discouraged her, and told many stories about my good pals Rhett Butler and Ernest Hemingway and all the large fish we had killed. Fresh and salt water. She loved me.

Hurricanes came and went. Water passed under lower Keys' bridges and I fattened on rum, lost the hair from most of the top of my head and a decade real quick. Folks I knew died, lots of them, mostly while they were not in bed having sex, and children became adults before my glassy, faulty, faded brown eyes. My wife remained young and beautiful. God loves her best.

When we opened our full-scale restaurant up the keys at mile marker ten, the Frenchman and his lady came up with us. It was a different adventure, full of the responsibilities of ownership and the onerous tasks of growing up. Bruno and his love bought a lovely thirty-four foot sloop with saved hot dog money and grit. They knew nothing about sailboats or sailing except it was cheaper than the rent and danger of living on Thomas Street. We marveled from the sidelines and continued to age. My thick proud mustache grayed completely one morning while I was outside showering, surrounded by a thick stand of banana trees. Matched the remaining hair.

I do not remember the moment I met Bean. It was in the very early '70s, during the Junior Jurassic era of this evolving island, when it was really like it should be here. Before, way before. I do remember who assigned us to be friends, and I thank him for it occasionally still, usually late at night. I have watched his beautiful children become savvy men with a gift for living, and he mine. So the friend thing has thickened in our latitude and as much as I can love a man, guess Bean is there. Low country boys can generally be trusted, even if they leave home. His father died an ideal death. I see that as family karma, and grin inside the privileged knowledge.

My great friend Nick once captained the skies, piloting seven-forty things through the stratosphere, arriving at all his destinations safely, a good thing. He trudged through the lonely stress of airborne life until its disagreement disengaged him and he became a captain of the oceans. I like him best at sea level. I call him the prototype for modern man and it is not a joke. Trust me.

Nick bought a new boat. Gleaming green and white twenty-five foot center console equipped for our waters and his fishing specialties. Nick stored the vessel dry at Oceanside Marina over on Stock Island. The Bean, Bruno and I were invited to one of the inaugural outings on July 26. We met at the docks at eight, admired the great new fishing toy, loaded it with too much in the way of supplies, most of it liquid, iced down in the hundred and fifty quart chest at the stern. Light beer mostly, and some candy and the lovely biscuits Lucy had Zip-locked for me the evening before. There was country ham between some of the biscuits.

Lucy mastered biscuits under the watchful eye of my grandmother, who will no doubt when the time arrives make God his biscuits. So there was nutrition aboard.

Bruno and I had never fished together, and the sport had evaded him completely until this fine morning. A chop came from the east that the Suzuki engine ate like it was melting. We cleared the main ship's channel and headed south to the Gulfstream to load the boat with dolphin. I sell them for profit at mile marker ten, grilled, fried, broiled or blackened. I popped a beer and licked my profit chops. Bruno would not forget this day, having never known the bedlam of a school of good-sized Dolphin, and I owed him some fun. I held on and grinned at the morning. Nick's sparkling new electronics indicated that the water beneath us was a tad over one thousand feet when we "spun a hub."

"Spinning a hub" is normally not that big a deal, as everyone knows. So there would be no problem. Sand Key was within sight and we could hopefully crawl slowly there and repair the prop and continue our way. Hour or so. More great light beer.

It was going real slow.

Nick and I were behind the console and its electronics, which were mounted above the steering station, he at the helm and me suddenly in ankle deep salt water behind and to his right.

"Bobby, throw the cooler overboard, quickly," Nick shouted.

Son of a bitch musta weighed two hundred fifty pounds. I threw it into the sea in a smooth single well coordinated motion like a feathered pillow. We were sinking. The loss of weight had no effect. Wet calves now. Nick ordered life jackets from the forward cabin, where the Bean and Bruno were stunning themselves. They threw me an orange life vest and slid one at Nick. The boat began to list seriously at its stern.

That last minute and a half was real crowded. Jumped into the ocean right after Bean and Bruno. Nick still aboard, vertical, giving Mayday coordinates to the airways. Shit hot captain.

What you do first here is a lot of laughing and heh heh heh stuff. Wow, no shit, looka here. Wow. Floating...

Then you look around and check out who you're with.

Nobody in this group is losing any cool. The former vessel's captain continues to do his work, telling us about sticking together near the remains of the completely vertical brand new boat, which we did. I could not believe how long he stayed aboard talking bunches of numbers repeatedly through the local airwaves. Three feet of bow pointing at heaven, gurgling strangely as it rode the waves with us. The intermittent laughing disbelief continued.

There was debris. Gas and oil on the waters surface, chum from the forward cooler, and just out of reach Lucy's lovely biscuits floated by zip locked in freshness headed for Sand Key Light and beyond. I'd lost my appetite.

We were floating in a chum line.

My great French pal Bruno offered out the side of his mouth, "So Bobby, how quickly the fisherman becomes the bait, no?"

We laughed some more as a five-pound box of frozen Ballyhoo floated past on its way to defrost.

There were several other setbacks. My life preserver was completely tangled so I slung one shoulder through it and captured a big orange buoy with fifteen feet of line or so and spread the line around. The seas were choppy and the morning had become quite gray. On the upside of the waves we could catch a glimpse of Sand Key, our intended destination. Looked nice and sea level. Dry.

We bobbed. I decided to leave my shoes on somewhere early in the proceedings. We had gone down inside two minutes. The adrenaline had been shrieking through since and let's face it, it's a serious drug, something to depend on. Leave it to the big guy to equip each of his earthly units with adrenaline as part of the hard drive. Nice touch.

It came to mind that we were in way over our heads. There were fairly big waves, and we were not the largest creatures in the pond. I missed my dead friend Mike and our innocent annual foolishness up in the shallow lakes and creeks of Georgia. I no longer missed any sort of sinking. On the plus side, my floating pals were the best. Nick, his take charge Russian genes at the forefront, techno man with a salt water gurgle, still the captain of our sea, and we listened. He be the man. Me and the Bean, southern and sinking, still smiling dead-eyed at one another, our strong collective sense of survival meshed, unafraid and sturdy, shared wordless in the salt. Bruno, the side of his French mouth cracking with acerbic frogisms and doubt of fishing in general, no longer on his to do list, also flaring a toothy grin. Four really cool guys just bobbing.

The whop whop whop of the choppers can be a symphony. Oh lord, what a sound. Glorious Federal sounds, whop whop whop.

They came by low, loud like Vietnam. Aggressive in grey.

Missed us completely. Flew by.

Waving like hysteria, wet to bone, feeling ironic and invisible.

Nick had done well with the airwaves. Jeff Burns heard the mayday, cut his charter's lines and told them to hang on. He'd written the coordinates in his palm when he heard the mayday.

He spotted us just after the chopper had missed us, radioed them and they whopped back above us. The waves were ferocious under the whip of the copter's blades, blowing us away from the boat hull and creating separation. The Navy dropped a diver in the water to assist us if necessary. Having Jeff now on the scene, we profusely thanked the jumper and opted for the quick safety of Jeff's Sportfisher. Never timid, I boarded first, someone had to do it. Nick came aboard last, every bit the captain still, and rarely lost sight of his boat's hull.

The fishing community here looks after one another. A forty-six foot Sportfisherman arrived next and I witnessed a boat birthing.

Nick and Jeff tied a strong line to the bow of the stricken vessel and the huge ship pulled Nick's new boat back on top of the ocean for him. Quite a sight.

We were transferred to two other boats on the return trip. We ended on the salvor's boat huddled together shocked still in the bow, four former bobbers. It was eleven o'clock. It had been a helluva morning.

Bruno had saved the backpack that has accompanied him around the world. He broke into it, pulled some dry fresh French bread and some brie and passed it around. We laughed again.

Lucy has requested I never begin another phone conversation with, "Are you sitting down?"

She caught me looking into the corner of the dark chocolate brown wall in our bedroom, a strange look on my face, several times.

I've stopped doing that now.

An Honorable Profession On A Greening Planet

BARBARA BOWERS

I up-anchored and sailed from Key West the day Summer died. No one blamed me for her death; a "freak accident" her trainer, Rebecca Marlow said. But somehow, Key West's luster faded with each early morning sunray that glistened on the little Pygmy Sperm whale's lifeless body.

When this least-understood-of-all-whale species washed ashore on June 21 — the new millennium's summer Solstice — I was among the core of locals who rallied to her side. Handling a wounded animal of any kind is a challenge, but baby Summer was an endangered species, maybe all of six weeks old.

She depended on us, volunteers who stayed in and out of the water with her, round the clock. Some of the regulars even camped out on site, and a Big Baby Nursery of sorts sprang up at the edge of the Salt Ponds.

We were always a quickly mobilized crew, but during the two-years I worked with Florida's Nature Rescue, none of us had participated in the rescue of an infant whale. Sure, there were plenty of turtles and dolphins, but never a prolonged effort to save the life of an animal as young and as rare as Summer. On-the-job training was the order of the day . . . and night, for she was never alone. Like any newborn, she needed constant attention. We supported her weight at the surface of the water to keep her blowhole above the waterline. We watched her every wiggle; when she burped, when she pooped, when she did any unremarkable thing we made notes.

We fashioned nipples for plastic-water-cum-baby bottles that we hoped would mimic her mother's teats. Initially, Summer ate every two hours. At first she drank a thick, milk mixture, of which the consistency was only guesswork. But little by little, squid gruel supplemented the milk formula, and eventually, our baby girl gained weight. We showered her with gifts: "noodle" toys to play with, beach balls, floats.

We stopped holding our breaths when Summer hit six-months . . . so little was known, then, about Pygmy Sperm whales. Only one had survived in captivity, and that one, only for four months. What do they eat? How do such deep-ocean going, solitary creatures find each other? And why was Summer abandoned in a shallow surf of rocks and corals that cut her baby soft skin?

Because female whales usually attend to their young for years, did Summer's mother die? Did she know something we didn't?

Throughout her short, ten months of life, Summer tested each of her surrogate nannies like any child might. When I traded out early morning shifts with Jean or Candace, she almost always tried to suckle my arm, an instinct that Rebecca tried to squelch: To survive the near-impossible odds of an orphaned whale, Summer had to learn that only her trainers were her food sources.

Each morning after the 4 a.m. shift switched over, Summer and I were alone in the makeshift, net encircled pen, playing bump-and-hide in the dark water. She was such a tease at dawn. Then, with the sun rising from behind the Atlantic Ocean and the moon setting behind the low-rising Key West skyline, Summer's short bursts of play always gave way to a remarkable calm. In the chilly water, a heart-warming trust settled over this stepmother-and-child-of-unlike-species: She'd lean her body into mine as I supported her at the water's surface. While she slept, I leaned my body into hers to listen to her quiet breath escape through her half-moon-shaped blowhole. Sometimes five, still minutes lapsed between her breaths. Her pectoral fin clasped my arm to the soft, silken skin of her breast. Her heart beat in my hand.

A young whale's heart beat in the palm of my hand.

Old Davies' chatter snaps me to attention. He's among the first Bequian locals I've met since leaving Key West in February. That's when I migrated to the Eastern Caribbean the same way whales head south in the winter to breed in warmer water. I had spied the spray from these gentle giants as my sailboat approached Bequia and while I wasn't necessarily eager for another encounter with such global citizens, wounds heal according to no one's Day-timer, and six weeks had passed since Summer died. My guilt was less; the "if-onlys" were fewer.

The lean, leathery waterman who is as creased and gray as the wooden oar he's mending on the beach tells me how a big bull almost dragged the boat down, and his buddies with it. He swears no one gets hurt, and Old Davies confides, "Day don't have 'nuff scope on 'de harpoon. Day only got wet dat day, an'de whale got away."

This is not a basic "big fish that got away" tale, and the man doing the "fishing" here probably won't show up soon on the cover of *Field and Stream*. He is no god and he doesn't walk on water, but on this palm-lined piece of paradise in the Grenadines, Athneal Ollivierre comes close: He walks on whaleback and that makes him legendary, if not immortal.

"Athneal only goes after humpbacks," said Davies matter-of-factly.

Unlike Hawaii where too many whale watchers "love them to death," in Bequia, this outdoor sport isn't quite so trendy: Death is the object. Even within the placid waters of Admiralty Bay, the island's natural harbor where I'm anchored amidst beaucoup yachts, a cow and her calf were harpooned in recent history.

Understanding the balance of man and nature is a precarious business, at best, and at this particular moment in my life, questions far outnumber answers. But something compels me to find out why a civilized, island community destroys humpbacks; creatures whose lucid songs drift in outer space for the next 20 million years in an effort to reach and interact with life in distant galaxies. In the scheme of things natural, their impact spans all geological eras. These mammals that went to sea 30 million years ago proliferated, then in one century, pouf, they barely endure man's onslaught.

Now, during an Ecological Golden Age, are Bequians completely out of sync with the universe? Environmentally illiterate? Are they starving?

"New England whalers, dey come to Bequia a hundred years ago," said Davies, absorbed with his oar and talking more to himself than to me. "Dey want Bequian waterman's help — we know des waters, mon — but we don't want dos damn Yankees, so Mr. Wallace, he starts up his own whalin' operation."

Today, while scientific study on humpback whales is internationally funded at the Dominican Republic's Silver Bank Sanctuary, just around the Caribbean corner Bequian natives, like Alaskan Eskimos, still hunt humpbacks. But in Bequia, one man embodies this fading nautical spirit more than most.

"Athneal Ollivierre," said the Whaleboner's bartender. The giant vertebrates made into bar stools and the huge ribs arching the entry explains the bar's name, and why this is a likely place to start my inquiry.

And of course, Old Davies knows with whom I should speak: "When you catch up to Athneal, tell 'im I said 'Hi.'"

But catching up to Athneal is akin to catching up to a whale: It takes persistence and a large amount of good timing. It's much easier to talk about whaling with someone else — everyone else — than it is to talk with him. During whaling season December through May, he and his crew are at sea or in "whale shacks" on Bequia or Mustique everyday at daybreak. No cell phones. No faxes. No interference from unwanted sources. Island time prevails in these parts, and if it's supposed to, things just happen. With communication links and time zones like this, you ease your way into a man's life.

From Port Elizabeth's tidy pavilion where locals wait for the island's small fleet of taxis, I notice the Police Chief, decked out in his starched khaki uniform on this warm spring morning. Bayshore Mall — all eight stores of it — is across the street, and some other shops flank the open-air market where tourists are targets for aggressive veggie hawkers. T-shirt and jewelry vendors splash the landscape near the pier with more color than ubiquitous bougainvilleas. And all this, just up the street from the wood-moldy depths of the New York Bar.

Here, I begin my harbor town stroll to its offbeat, residential left bank where I meet Portia and Shanita. They're out of school for the Easter holiday, just like that February Sunday when the whale was killed.

"I didn't get to see it," said 11-year old Portia, disappointment written all over her ebony face. "Everybody else watched but me."

I'm shocked that a pretty, young girl wanted to see a whale killed. Wouldn't you rather see it alive? Watch it breach, or take photos?

She's clearly perplexed with my questions about whales, but Portia makes herself quite clear about Bequia and its whaling men: "Everybody stops what they're doing to watch. It's like carnival; it's fun. And it's dangerous, and they're very brave men."

In case I missed that, Shanita steps in front of me, looks down at her shiny, patent leather Easter shoes and repeats, "Very brave."

The whale harpooned six weeks ago was the first one taken in four years, and the "very brave" men who killed it rekindled a celebration of yesteryear wherein thousands of people lined the shore to watch the chase in progress. The distribution of its booty, which took an unprecedented two hours to butcher, was broadcast over the radio for all St. Vincent and the

Grenadines to hear. As Old Davies puts it, this "joy dat comes to 'de whole island when a whale is harpooned," has generally given way to tamer events such as the upcoming Easter Regatta and fishing tournament.

Of course, dead fish are major sporting events in Key West, too, where pirates of yore have donned leisure suits and squirmed into the white-collared tourist trade. With big boats and big bucks, they swarm the Keys' Windex-blue water in search of bonefish and tarpon and marlin, but even there, dying whales are not synonymous with joy. Truth is, friends tell me the entire Florida Keys mourned the day that Summer died; the morning she played with me, her trusted babysitter. The morning she dived underwater and was trapped in a hole in the net. If only I reacted sooner. If only we had repaired that net more carefully. If only, if only.

The next day, I intend to hike from Port Elizabeth across Bequia's humpbacked spine, two miles to Friendship Bay. At a crossroads of the island's summit, I meet Narris sitting in the shade of a taxi pavilion. His Land Rover sits idly in the blazing sun. He dickers a deal: "Buy my service, lady, an' I will show you all of South Bequia."

There I will find not only the new airport under construction, but also the Moonhole, which is possibly a resort, but mostly a mystery to the islanders. Because it is "much too far to walk, maybe t'ree miles," I need Narris. What's more, I need Eddy, who will be my personal guide, no extra charge. The pot is further sweetened with a stop in La Pompe at Athneal's house on the return to Friendship Bay.

Had the accent been different, I'd swear Narris is a used car salesman from New Jersey.

The curvaceous ride south is breathtaking. Palm trees, papaya, flamboyant, white cedar, fig trees and more sway wildly in the easterly winds like an unrehearsed chorus line. Gold sand ribbons lace the jungle's edge, and a sandy, gauze-like petticoat surrounds the shallows of nearby Petty Nevis, a small, uninhabited island used only by whalers for the past century. Mother Nature's femininity camouflages mankind's masculinity here, where hand winches recently hoisted a 35-foot humpback. Gaffs, lances and other near-antique tools butchered its meat and blubber, and contained its oil. Here, an eternity of beauty, and a century of tradition clash with the new airport, soon to open — soon to jar Bequia into the age of mass tourism.

The airport is built along this ruggedly beautiful coast at Paget Farm because it is flat. With land reclamation from the shallows, it sports a modern terminal for small, inter-island aircraft. Quick trips from neighboring St. Vincent will increase visitors who, until now, only traveled to Bequia via ferryboat or private yacht.

"The banana market has dried up. Fishing and boat building are declining. Whaling's almost gone," said Eddy Friday, my afternoon guide, who, like many of the Caribbean's best and brightest, left traditional island jobs for more lucrative posts as taxi drivers and tourist guides. "Tourism is our economic mainstay, and the airport will fast forward its development."

Tom Reston is unsure how the airport will affect the Moonhole, a superb collection of private homes built into the rock cliffs of southern Bequia. They are occasionally rented to visitors, hence, the confusion about the Moonhole being a resort. Tom, whom I surprised by my visit to this remote part of the island, manages the property when he's not directing his Grenadines Film Company. He doesn't have time now, but Tom will meet me tomorrow to talk about the documentary he's been filming for five years; the one about whaling.

En route to Friendship Bay, as promised, Narris stops at Athneal's home overlooking the bay and Petty Nevis. It's late afternoon; no one is home. Two trim, middle-aged men walking the narrow roadway past Athneal's tell me he's in from work, but gone to town. "Try around 5 o'clock," they say.

When I get back in the taxi, Eddy proudly announces, "They're two of Athneal's whaling crew."

At the Friendship Bay Hotel I finally reach Athneal by phone. I can drop by his home the next day at 5:00, and as I walk Friendship Bay, a few miles from the airport and just around the bend from Petty Nevis, I find a massive, three-foot long bone fragment that must weigh ten pounds. Washed ashore, it's a whale bone, maybe part of a rib, and it produces mixed feelings about Lars Conradsen's prediction: "The whale killed in February will be the last one harpooned the Old Way," said the bearded hotel owner.

He was holding his twin girls in his lap, and chatting leisurely with guests in his restaurant. "Moby Dick was hunted and harpooned the Old Way." But Lars pointed out a big difference. "Moby was a sperm whale, and Bequians don't hunt Cap'n Ahab's mortal enemy. They hunt only humpies, for the meat is tastier and more beef-like than sperm whales."

Though no one commented, another big difference was understood: Unlike mechanized commercial methods that decimated whale populations worldwide by the 1940's, whaling the Old Way pits fewer than seven men in an open, 26-foot boat against as much as 40 tons of whale; against an animal that may be 800 times the size of a man.

"These are locally built boats with no motors. They are ballast filled, and after spotters in whale shacks signal the whale's direction, Athneal takes up the chase with his men, using long oars and sails only." One of the twins started crying, and Lars bounced her gently on his knee, too much into his story to stop now: "When the whale is within striking distance, perhaps 15 yards, Athneal physically throws the harpoon, with a rope attached to it, into the whale. Then for the next few hours, the whaleboat and crew go for the Nantucket sleigh ride taught them by New England whalers."

"De first blow rarely kills 'de whale," chimed in Big Jack, a regular at the outdoor bar. "Course, Athneal is 'de only mon who's killed a 50-foot whale with a single harpoon thrust dat pierced its heart."

Wounds from lances repeatedly thrown into the whale take their toll, and when Athneal decides the time is right, he walks on the whale's back to a vulnerable spot and sinks the final blow. Long believed a heroic feat that died with New England whalers and the Old Way of whaling, Athneal's intimate combat with the humpback in February was caught on film.

"Some of the whalers thought I was the jinx," said Tom Reston. We're in his two-room, tropically patina-ed film studio, sans high-tech gear like telephones or glass windows. "I've been filming their work for four years, and from the time I started, they hadn't caught a whale 'til now. They're very superstitious men."

But Tom points out no whales have been taken in four years because Athneal retired from whaling. In this, his first season back, a whale was slain. The actual death of a whale is missing from *Easterlies That Blow*, but even in this unfinished state, Tom's cinematography is excellent. And as Athneal affirms an hour later, many of his sensitive interviews reflect Athneal's own concern — few men are following in his footsteps.

The half hour hike to the master whaler's home makes me late; the long workday and the late afternoon hour make him sleepy. Athneal is dozing in a lawn chair when I climb the stairway to his patio. Trailways, a mongrel with more seniority than Athneal, is on guard. Sitting down on a step next to the dog, and not far from the whaler, we three size each other up. I know immediately I like Athneal: A giant killer with a no-breed mutt can't be all bad.

Athneal came out of retirement this year because he doesn't want whaling, largely a family endeavor, ended in Bequia. "Day don' catch whales for four years 'cause I quit," said the dark-skinned man in a silky English Creole who seems, himself, to be a gentle giant. "Y'am training two men now."

One of them is an Ollivierre, Athneal's third cousin. His uncle and mentor, Jonston, set Athneal up with his first whaleboat 47 years ago. He died shortly after Athneal stunned everyone by killing a humpback with a single harpoon thrust to its heart.

As he talks, I feel the pound of Summer's heartbeat against the palm of my hand, and I try hard to understand this man. He explains the hazards of the job, "no health insurance; no safety nets." He details the difficulty of lancing a whale; how tough it was to step down. Perhaps my expression shows; perhaps he senses my pain, but for some reason he lightens up. He begins mocking the aging process. He assures me, I too, will grow up and understand the ways of the world, the sometimes-cruel twists of day-to-day living. Yes, even I will develop "old shakin' hands; do I plan to work 'de next season," teases the graying whaler who looks years younger than 70. "Maybe 'de next year, too."

Athneal says he and his men are conscious of the humpback's plight, he has seen the numbers decrease as his years increased as a whaler. But the three whales Bequians are limited to catching each season has little effect upon the endurance of the species.

"Humpbacks are makin' a comeback," said Athneal with the certainty of a marine biologist who just completed the latest census. What really worries Athneal, though, is there will be no one 'der to thin 'dem out like deers."

Walking me through a lifetime of memorabilia — whale bone furniture; a mobile of all the whale species hanging next to a painting of him on whaleback; photos with Bequian dignitaries — the name of his whaleboat "Why Ask" is suddenly clear, charming and a testimony to his subtle humor. But the future of whaling is not clear to him, nor does it hold much humor. "It's hard work," he said. "It's 'de only death dat brings joy."

This year's whaling season is closing, only a few weeks left. I have hashed and rehashed the "joys" of whaling, the pain of dying. Rebecca sent me a copy of Summer's autopsy and it resurrects my sorrow; my cry for help when she didn't resurface from her dive. The anguish of her limp body tangled in the net. How we tried to resuscitate what we thought was a drowned whale, but was actually one who died from asphyxiation.

Within five minutes, a time frame in which she had easily held her breath during other play periods, excess carbon dioxide left Summer unconscious. She didn't have water in her lungs. The bump on her head, which grew slowly, and became more apparent each day of her young life, was the culprit.

We used to kid about her deformity. "She's Flipper, the first whale-dolphin hybrid." But apparently, this air bubble on her sinuses was a death sentence from birth. Summer's mother probably knew she could never dive with other Pygmy Sperm whales, and she pushed her imperfect baby up on Fort Zach's rocky beach that summer morning to die. Inadvertently, another species intervened until February 10, 2000 — the same day a humpback harpooned in Bequia momentarily resuscitated a slowly dying nautical heritage.

When I sail out of Admiralty Bay, past Bequia and across the channel on a northerly tack toward Key West, the slap of mighty flukes on water gets my attention. This time, I wonder if the endangered species isn't really humpback whalers.

Versions of Violet

MARGIT BISZTRAY

How did she get here, Violet wonders. In general, she knows. How many times has she been asked "What made you come to Key West?" More times than she's been asked her name.

By now the answer comes easily. She tells the short version. It goes something like this: "I grabbed my suitcase, held my son's hand, and with a baby in my belly, stepped off a cruise ship leaving a cheater of a boyfriend." Occasionally, she will disintegrate around the word "cheater." Lousy, fucking, worthless, lying. It makes her sound tougher, more recovered. This is the way she'd like to be, like the leather pants she'd wear if she was somebody different. Each time she tells the short version, a lump forms in her throat. Of course, there's much more to the story. More than a sentence brought her to Key West and to the front porch of her house, where she sits sipping her con leche. Sometimes she thinks about the long version.

Ginger, who lives next door, calls everything that takes place in her life "more material." If she finds a scorpion under her sink, that's more material. Three days of rain and a flooded yard is more material. Even the abortion she had was more material. This is because Ginger works three days in a bookstore, then does what she calls "dancing" those same three nights so she can be who she really is the other four days a week. To most people, Ginger is a stripper, but Ginger says she is a writer who dances. Her book is titled *Present Perfect.* Its narrator is loosely based on Ginger herself, Ginger admits, because her life is blessed with interesting material. This character dances as well, but really wants to write poetry. Then one day one of her customers reveals he is a literary agent, reads her work and deems it the next big thing. He has it published and Oprah selects it for her book club. Much to Ginger's surprise, the agent and the dancer fall in love and get married. She hadn't anticipated that twist in the plot; it simply happened.

Ginger survives on fig bars and cranberry ginger ale. By Thursday, her bin gleams with empty cans, but just before the recycling truck comes, a silent man named Tornado arrives. He wears a black, woolen suit and a pair of boots. His long beard is yellow with oil slicks of gray. Over his shoulder, he carries a large, plastic bag, and once he empties Ginger's cans into its opening, he walks out to Stock Island, four miles away, and sells the cans for a little money.

A cab driver told Violet Tornado used to talk. He used to stand on Duval street and yell how he was blown here from Missouri by a tornado, and lots of other bull. Then he got beat up and had his voice box crushed, and shut the hell up. Those were the cabbie's words. Of course, who knows the truth. Tornado must have a long version too, stored in his silent self.

After Tornado leaves, Violet hears the recycling truck growling at the top of her street. This is her sign to get up. Her quiet morning is over. She stands and stretches. Before she enters her house, she sighs. At some point, she and Mickey agreed they wouldn't try too hard to keep the house too clean. Mickey works all day as a legal clerk and Violet sells shells and tries to be a good mother. At day's end, they're tired. They'd rather not keep house. They'd rather play. After the kids are in bed, they order pizza and listen to old Rolling Stones albums. They watch Animal Planet on mute, and take turns narrating, complete with sound effects. They play with Mickey's Polaroid, pinning their faces next to those of models torn out of Details and Vogue. Sometimes, they dance.

Night after night of fun adds up to mess. A mess of wrappers, torn magazines, glasses, food cartons, Polaroids, chocolate chip cookie crumbs and condom wrappers clutters the living room. It is a mess of things already gone, and it's quite a mess. Violet surveys it, then drags a Shell Shack shirt out from beneath a chair, sniffs it and puts it on.

"Bye!" she calls. "Love you!"

Through the tunnel of her house, she sees the ones she loves like an arrangement of light sculptures. The back door illuminates them, as if they're trying on sunlight and it fits perfectly. Joseph's curly, bamboo-colored hair glints above his high chair. Mickey's shadow cradles the body of Haley, curled like a shrimp in his lap. Her bottle slopes in his hand, siphoning light into the blossom of her mouth.

Mickey gives the kids breakfast in order to allow Violet to sit on her porch and drink her coffee alone. She doesn't know why Mickey offers this, or why he cares for her. She has an ordinary job that barely covers the nanny. She has two children in diapers, fathered by someone she nicely calls a cheater. Mickey knows Violet isn't tough. Her story's boring and short and Mickey doesn't know the long version. He's never asked because he loves her the way she is, of course. This is confusing, but comforting. Violet has pretty hair, but then, so do cats. Stretch marks and cellulite and wrinkles have moved in like new territories, suddenly discovered on her map. When she met Mickey seven months ago, she was still breastfeeding Haley. Her breasts hurt like a wandering toothache, and she told Mickey Don't Touch. He hung around, much to her surprise. The cheater wouldn't have. This fact alone made Mickey good enough.

Still, there is the question How did she get here? On recent mornings, she's wondered, because it's been almost a year now. The day is vivid as pink bougainvillea, still. The sun fell on the gangplank like lollipops. It was a gorgeous day. She was phenomenal and strong. She'd heard a woman described like that on television: phenomenal and strong. Violet had walked, no she had strode, down that gangplank, phenomenal and strong. She'd hummed goodbye cheater, goodbye, goodbye. She'd fairly sung the word, hadn't she? Wasn't she thrilled that day? Wasn't she positively thrilled?

First, she called her mother in Maryland collect. "I left him, mom, just like you said I should." That's what she'd planned to say. But then her mother announced "Your grandma Violet died. We couldn't reach you."

Violet almost protested. The ship's emergency phone number! The fax machine! Violet had e-mail, but her mother didn't believe e-mail worked.

"She left you her money. She wasn't rich, but she was smart with her cash."

Which Violet wasn't, of course. This was implied. Mother was good at implying things.

"She always bought you the best. You were her namesake. She had expected great things from you."

Again implying the opposite. Violet had never been great at much.

"I'll put the money into your bank account. It's yours to do with what you please."

Violet wandered the streets of Key West that day, pregnant and sad. She fed Joseph popsicles to keep him quiet, but he whined anyway. She missed her grandmother terribly. All day, she heard the sentence "Don't be a lady, Violet. Be a good woman." It was her grandmother's motto. Violet twisted the jade ring on her finger, the one from her grandmother, and tried to be strong. The spark of stepping off the cruise ship had disappeared. She wasn't strong or phenomenal, she was just scared. She bought the house and moved in and got a job at the Shell Shack.

Biking to work, she sees the woman who sweeps clean the sidewalk in front of her house with a freshly cut palm frond. A pack of orange geckos climbs to the roof of the welder's house. The golden-brown man in white shorts walks his white poodle. The postal worker does his t'ai chi next to the mango tree. It is a usual morning. Violet pulls up at ten to nine.

Ricardo and Smith arrived a moment earlier, looking hungover. Violet sees Betty opening the door for them. Betty has worked for the company for years and has an office job. She isn't seen around the Shell Shack except on payday. It isn't payday.

"Hey Betty. What a surprise," she says.

"Good morning, Violet," Betty says. She doesn't smile, which is unusual. Betty always smiles, having won the prize of working for Traditional Tours nearly half her life. When she had managed the Shell Shack, museum, ice cream stand and beach shop, Betty had almost seemed powerful. She hired Violet a week before her transfer to the office, chatting with pride about her status in the company. Violet had listened with dull disinterest, thinking Dear god, don't let me end up like her. Betty was boring, but so? The job was safe, like solid ground at the bottom of a gangplank.

Betty flicks on the fluorescent lights and plugs in the cash register. Violet and Smith exchange looks.

"Starfish go there." Betty points.

"They got in people's way," says Smith.

"Starfish go there. There's where they sell. One of you, put them back."

Betty picks up a fallen mobile. "Place is a wreck," she clucks.

"What are you doing here?" asks Smith.

"I'm at the register again. You're on the floor and in the back helping Ricardo. Soon as season's over, you each get cut a day."

Smith looks surprised, then shrugs. "I'll help Ricardo."

Violet digs one hand into her hip. "No one told us that!"

"Violet, I just told you. What, you forget already?"

"I mean before. I mean, this isn't professional!"

"Violet, don't tell me what's professional. I've been here twenty years. I'm fifty-seven years old. Yesterday, I learn a guy's been hired for my job. He has a business degree. All I can do is what I've done for twenty years, which is to work for this company."

"But it's not fair! You must have rights?" Violet hears her voice shake, feels all her fingers shake.

Betty's hand flutters around her face. "I don't understand that stuff, Violet. I know they cut my pay, which means I have to work more hours. I got my son living at home. I got a mother with diabetes. With my seniority here, I get the hours I want. That's why they're cutting you and Smith."

Betty is proud of her seniority. She's often said so. But now, she looks tired and old.

"My boyfriend works for a lawyer, Betty. I'll get his advice."

Betty turns away. "Just put the starfish back, Violet. Unlock the door."

Violet fidgets through the morning. Cruise ship passengers with sunburns arrive in a hurry, arguing about what gifts they need to buy. They part with money as if it were flesh, count the change with an expression of regret. She can't believe she used to live with them. She used to sit in the piano lounge, angry that he was singing them the words he used to sing only to her. They are the people who stole her words, and she dislikes them with all her heart. But there is more. Part of herself was left behind on that cruise ship, too. Sometimes she searches the passengers, hoping to snatch it from their grip. It's an important part. She was phenomenal and strong! She must have dropped it on the gangplank and someone else picked it up.

When she arrives back home, Violet meets Ginger, who has just kissed goodbye an Asian man wearing a business suit.

"Hey, Violet," she says, clutching the folds of her kimono, a deep, seashell pink. Her fingernails match the kimono.

"Japanese?" Violet asks, jerking her head in the direction the man has gone.

"Yeah, Japanese are sweet. I've got one in my book."

She pops a cranberry ginger ale and leans against her gate. "So how's it going with you?"

Violet pauses. She and Ginger talk, but they don't talk about big things. They talk about movie stars, crimes and ways to turn on a man. Maybe she ought to try the truth, try out a long version.

"Something unfair happened at work today. I'm fuming over it."

Ginger jerks her hand to her ear, spilling her gingerale. “Whoa, stop! Stop! Stop!” She takes a slurp from her can. “I can’t absorb negative energy.” She waits a moment for this to sink in. “Writers feel more than average people, Violet. I’m at a deep part of my book, right where the dancer and the agent fall in love. I have to keep myself surrounded in love so I can stay in that space, you see.”

Violet waits, but that’s it.

“Well, when you’re done with that part, maybe we’ll talk.”

Ginger’s expression holds still, as though her tank just got flushed.

“Maybe, okay. I’ve only been at this part a few months, but...”

She sips her gingerale again. Then from her pocket she draws out a business card.

“Here, call my friend Toni. Get a massage. Bring the love back.”

Violet takes the card. “Thanks.”

“No problem, sure,” says Ginger, tossing her can into the empty recycling bin. “It’s all material, you know.”

Violet waves. It’s not material to her. But then, what is it?

She slams her gate and feels a lump rise in her throat. It is the beast finding its way out of the cave. It’s Violet’s voice.

She kicks a pizza box inside the door. Did they agree not to keep house? Now she’s not sure.

“Clean up this mess!” she yells, although there’s nobody at home. Since there is nobody at home, she yells more. She yells until her throat clears, and then she laughs.

When Mickey pulls up in his old Mercedes Benz, Violet is stomping on trash bags to fit them in the cans. “You cleaning house, babe?” he says. Poor thing. He has no idea.

“What does it look like?"

“Looks like you need a night out. How about a restaurant?”

“You said you’d trim the bougainvillea. You said you’d fix the porch swing.”

Mickey stands outside the gate. “You get your period today?”

“Ha!” Violet laughs.

Mickey does not react. It didn’t sound like real laughter.

“Am I a lady, or am I good woman?”

“I think you’re good,” he says. “I like you, anyway.”

“Then why’d he lie to me, Mickey? There I was pregnant with his child, holding his son. He told more lies than there were lifeboats on that ship."

Violet twists her jade ring, and then tells Mickey the long version. She tells him all about the songs, about the day her singer told her she was fat, about the pretty, Norwegian activities director who wasn't fat.

"He was the love of my life," she says, finally. "You need to know this much."

Mickey turns away, a little. Then he turns back again.

"Can I come home, or are you breaking up?"

She stares at him a moment, the man at her gate. It never seemed as though he knew her, but now he does. He knows, and still he wants to come home. Maybe she is not only strong and phenomenal, but loveable as well. Could it be true? Perhaps she's stepped onto the gangplank intact this time, all her possessions clutched to her heart.

"You gonna trim that bougainvillea and fix that swing?"

"I will, Violet."

"And no more mess in the living room."

Mickey unlatches the gate. He lines the trash cans in a row along the fence. Violet watches him. She sees he does this not to please her, but because he's changed. He's changed a tiny little bit, and it is plenty.

"How was work today?" he asks.

"I need to talk to Leland. I need to ask about some laws. Laws on employment, demotions. Stuff I don't know what's called, but there are laws for it, I know that."

"Okay. I'll help whatever way I can."

The doors to the nanny's minivan slide open and shut. The sounds of her children flutter in the air. Joseph is chattering away. Carmen speaks back to him in Spanish, words that sound dipped in hot pink. Joseph's chubby hand juts through the fence, a soft claw she wants to kiss. He is so precious to her! And there is Haley, riding the swing of Carmen's arm. Her face jumps for joy at the sight of Violet. Her arms reach for her mother, and Violet runs to her. Carmen is cooing in Spanish as Violet pulls her children tightly to her heart and holds them, saying their names. As she bids Carmen goodbye she turns, carrying Haley and holding Joseph's hand. The sun is glazing the spindles of her front porch like lollipops.

THE TENANT

ROSALIND BRACKENBURY

She wanted something, he'd known it straight off: a room in his house, his life, his heart. He should have said no from the get-go. But Linda was already showing them round, the pale thin young woman with the bowed shoulders and the darting glance, and the woman who had brought her here, who was an artist. The artist had red nails and frizzed, dyed orange hair and brightly colored clothes. She was about seventy; you could see from her hands, the patient hands of an old craftswoman not really disguised by the nails, the paint. She had lived in Paris, oh yes. Adored it. Those were the days. She knew people. She flicked ash from her cigarette and dropped names. Of course, they'd know, they were artists, she'd heard. They would know that artists, true artists, had to help each other. Take poor Lacey, for example, who was having to leave her apartment at the end of the week, such a terrible story, they would die when they heard it, and now she had nowhere to live. They had an apartment, didn't they? Or a room, at least. They were artists, writers, they knew how it was.

"She's an artist?" he asked vaguely, thinking of pots of paint up there, heavy sculptures that might come through the floor.

"Well, she has the temperament." The old artist, who might also have the temperament but did have those hands to back her up, spoke as if pale Lacey were not there. "She writes a bit. You are writers, you will get on so well."

Temperament without talent, Abe thought, a bad mixture. She writes a bit, does she?

But Linda and the two women were moving away from the little table in the shade where they'd drunk their coffee, the artist exclaiming about its excellence, delicious, wonderful, how do you do it? Just Cuban, Linda told her, in an Italian pot; we like it strong.

He couldn't see that any of this mattered. Why was it happening? Perhaps in a minute something else would happen, some siren would scream down the street, or a cell phone would ring, a knock come at the door, and the two visitors would be whisked away. He didn't want to have to do anything about them, one way or the other. He wanted his morning peace, and for life to be as it had been before they appeared.

Linda led the way round the side of the house, where the uneasy staircase went up to the apartment. She'd already shown them each plant she and Abe had planted in the yard, the hibiscus, the bougainvillea against the fence, the new Christmas tree palm that was going to block off the view of the house at the back of them. Abe sat and finished his coffee. It wasn't necessary, he thought, to show people plants like that. Everyone had plants. Or rather, plants were everywhere, they didn't have to be introduced. He'd been in the tropics for twenty-five years, though, and to Linda it was all new and extraordinary. They'd been married a month. He didn't trust this exclaiming about things, this showing strangers everything they had. The artist had left lipstick on the coffee mug, a red smudge on white china, and red ends on the cigarette butts in the ashtray. She was someone who expected to be liked; expected, yes, to be obeyed. Women like that, exclaiming, flirting — he could hear her on the stairs, the little cry of admiration at the door of the apartment, the murmur of voices as the three women moved about up there. He should go up there and tell them all, it isn't available. But he sat still, tasted the cool dregs of his coffee, smoked, waited for some tumult to calm down in his brain. Sometimes, just doing nothing worked. He surveyed his yard, where the green shade had only begun to grow back after his pruning — the areca palms, elephants' ears, crotons, and the new plants that would grow big and shield them in future years. From what? The encroachment he felt all around him — more people, more traffic, more money, more of everything except space and peace. Rats, he had read, got angry if too many other rats lived close around them. Scientists experimented on them, read their moods, peered into their tiny agitated brains. He was glad sometimes that nobody could see inside his brain.

They'd perched on their old metal chairs that morning, looking around them at it all. The house was raw still from their moving in, bare where they'd cleared debris away, like a person with a new haircut. And here was this strange woman, this Lacey person, demanding a way into their life, his and Linda's, and all he could do it seemed was let her have it.

They came downstairs. The artist, picking her way in high-heeled mules across the scraggly grass, Lacey hanging close to her like an uncertain child, Linda raising her eyebrows at him from behind them, in a way that he knew already from his brief life with her meant, "Please don't object to something I have already decided to do."

"It's so perfect," the artist said. "Just darling. There's a lot of work to do, of course, but it's so wonderfully bohemian, it would suit her down to the ground. Wouldn't it, Lacey?"

Pale Lacey spoke, her hands twisting together. "I could even help you, you know, fix it up, if you like. I've lots of experience. People say I have a very good design sense. People in New York often wanted me to fix up their places for them."

"A couple of weeks," Abe said, "We can probably help you out for a couple of weeks. But we have stuff to do up there, so no more."

When you know you're not doing the right thing, your stomach feels it, he knew. But then sometimes you override that visceral thing and do it anyway. Why? Because some old string has been tugged, some feeling hooked in you, and you are unable to say no.

He checked this out with Linda.

"I know. I felt uneasy too. From the beginning."

"Then why?"

"We have so much. We have a house, a life, each other. You know, having an extra room, a whole apartment up there. And it's so impossible to find anywhere, in Key West."

It was too late. They watched her move in. A man drove her with her possessions in a van. They watched the unknown man go up and down the rickety stairs to the attic, bent under Lacey's stuff, all that warm afternoon. Lacey herself waved her thin white hands and told him where to put things, what to do next. She didn't look fragile, not while she was telling someone what to do.

There was something going on in the house, even before Lacey stopped paying the rent, even before the accusations began. It was a feeling, as if something seeped through the ceiling from the room above. Linda and Abe began snapping at each other, then quarrelling. They barked sharp injurious words at each other, looked at each other in horror, tried to mend the harm. Then it began again. Sentences beginning "You always" and "You never" began to come out of their mouths. They apologized, Linda cried, Abe brought in handfuls of bougainvillea, blood-colored, to drop its petals around their bedroom. In bed they lay wakeful, eyes wide open and staring up to the ceiling, where Lacey was, invisible and silent, the quietest of tenants, but unarguably there. If they moved together, if they made love, she would be up there, above them. She never went out.

"What d'you think she's doing up there?"

"D'you think she's died?"

"D'you think she's all right? D'you think we should go and see?"

Then the rent stopped.

"We'll have to evict her. This is absurd."

"How do you do that?"

"I dunno. There's a procedure, you just follow the steps."

If only this were true, he thought, about other areas of life.

Abe went down to City Hall and got the booklet about evicting people. There were, as he had said, steps you had to follow, set periods of time between the steps. Linda thought, it's going to take more than this. She also thought, this is so bald, so brutal, surely I can find another way. She went and knocked on the upstairs door. Perhaps, as woman to woman, they could come to some agreement. After a long silence, Lacey came to the door. She opened it narrowly and her pale pointed face looked round it. Behind her, there were cardboard boxes, trunks, stuff piled high. A broadfaced cat, evidently male, stared from his place on the topmost box.

"Hi," Linda said, as pleasantly as she could. "You know, if you don't pay the rent, Lacey, we're going to have to evict you. You know, we did you a favor in making it so low."

"Are you giving me notice of eviction? Is that what you're saying?"

"No, I'm just kind of warning you, informally. I want you to know, you know, what'll happen, if you don't pay."

"I'm perfectly aware of my rights in law" was what Lacey said. What Linda heard, as she told Abe later, was a wail from inside the room, like an abandoned cat.

"Was the cat there?" he asked.

"Yes. I don't think the wretched animal's ever allowed out. Oh, God, Abe, I'm afraid we're in deeper than we think."

"Nah, there's a routine for dealing with this, it happens all the time.

Landlord tenant stuff. It's always going wrong. We just follow the rules."

What happened was that they began taking turns to be the bad guy. One day it was Abe who threatened, Linda who cajoled. Then they switched roles.

"Well, I've always believed really, property is theft."

"You mean, if you own a house, you're so wicked, you have to have someone living in the attic for free, just to bug you, just to make things right? Come on, Linda, that's nuts."

"Well, no, but you know, honey, she doesn't have anywhere to go, the world can be a grim place if you're homeless, maybe she's just temporarily broke, we don't know."

"So we have to put up with a goddamn succubus up there, just so's we're not grinding the faces of the poor?"

"No, not exactly, but hey, let's just give her the benefit of the doubt, I mean, eviction's a brutal way to go."

"You know, I think you're the one who's going insane."

Then they traded places.

"Linda, that poor woman up there, gee, all she wants from us is a little friendship, a little support. You're so hard on her. Anyway, I thought we agreed, a cash relationship is a lousy one to have with any human being. Maybe she's just hanging out for us to show her a little humanity, a little caring."

"Well, if you're so fucking caring, you just go up there and tell her she can stay for the rest of her damn life, she can rot up there for all I care."

So it went. Abe slammed the door and went out to check the outboard on his boat. Linda went into the yard where the mangoes rushed down through leaves and thumped to earth around her, and cried. The curtains of the upstairs room may or may not have twitched aside when Linda looked up; that blur at the window may or may not have been a face.

When Abe came back from the boat and the temperature had dropped a couple of degrees and they were drinking ginger ale with ice out on the back porch, they looked at each other with love and remorse. What could be done?

"She has to go," Abe said, "She's screwing up our lives, just by being there. I don't know how she's doing it, but she is."

"But we have to wait for the eviction process. Look, it says this number of days."

"I know. So let's stay sane, okay? Let's ignore her, let's pretend she's not there."

"Okay. I love you, honey."

"I love you."

Then the letters began arriving, in the mailbox, pushed under the door, tucked into the jalousies of the window in Abe's den. Handwritten in black ink on a yellow legal pad, as if to remind them that this was not about feelings but about the processes of law. Accusations. Steps, down into some basement of life from which there was no easy escape. On the 9th you did this, on the 11th you did that. On the 12th you were seen leaving the house. ..

Amazed, Abe read phrases out to Linda. "She thinks we're tapping her phone. She's heard sounds on the line. Why the hell would we want to do that?"

"She's insane."

"There's more. She thinks I've been in there and tampered with her computer and that's why she isn't getting any commissions."

"Commissions?"

"I know. Airhead stuff. Oh. She says she's going to take us to court."

"She's going to take us to court? Well, how can she? What for?"

"Ruining her life, she says."

"Can you sue someone for that? Jesus, if you could, I'd sue her for ruining ours."

"Listen to this. ' You are not the first people to treat me this way, but I will make sure you are the last.'"

"I think we need an exorcist, not a bailiff."

That night, in the heat of summer, they lay separate and sweating under the ceiling fan, awake, not talking, each listening to slight creaking sounds overhead.

"She's up. She's doing something." Abe whispered at last.

"This is like 'Gaslight'. You know? You can drive someone crazy just by being overhead."

"She's probably too hot. At least she hasn't said she's going to sue us for the heat."

"God, I'm sick of this. D'you realize, we never talk about anything these days but her? What she's doing, what she's not doing, those damn letters, what she might be going to do?"

"Yeah, we do, we talk of plenty of other things."

"We do not."

"We do so."

"We do not!" She turned on her side, naked, crying. Abe stayed flat on his back, gazing up through darkness like a man on a tomb, wondering how his life, which had seemed quite simple, had brought him to this.

He wanted to tell the judge everything, it was the only way. To confess, so that it would all be over. To tell him about poor Lacey, how she had a long history of bad relationships, landlords, boyfriends, her family; how she'd been an unwanted baby, an unloved child; pale, not strong, a girl alone in a hostile world, vulnerable, maybe even abused; how no one had recognized her talents, how her life had gone wrong from the outset. To plead for mercy, to be told it was not his fault. He was just an ordinary man, for God's sake. He couldn't do it. It wasn't his job, was it? You couldn't do this, nobody could have done it. Surely he was not guilty. In his dream he was begging the judge for mercy.

"Abe?" It was Linda, her hand on his sweaty back. "What is it? Are you dreaming?"

"Dreaming, yeah. Courtroom. Judge."

"What was happening?"

He rubbed his head, wiped sweat from his eyes. The fan turned above them, making the only air there was.

"Hey," he said, "D'you think I'm innocent?"

"Yes, I know you are."

In the darkness, silent and not touching but together, they both thought about what happens when you are asked for too much, when what's expected goes way beyond what's humanly possible.

"What do you think the judge will say?"

"I think he'll dismiss the case. I think he'll think she's nuts."

"I think so too."

"But it's me," he said, "What I seem to expect of myself, that bothers me."

"You know she's taken photos of the termite damage, the stained sink, the cracks in the floor? Not of the bougainvillea or the patterns the mango leaves make on the sky. Don't you think that's sad?"

"So, is there any truth in these accusations?" The judge is asking Abe, and it's a very hot morning, June in Key West; only in here it seems to be the air conditioning, the numb cold of it, that's making Abe sleepy. "Plaintiff says that you — ah — took a part out of her computer, that you thus made her unable to earn a living. Also that you tapped her phone and listened to her private calls. And that, yes, you made her cat sick. Is any of this true?"

Abe smiles at the judge. "No. None of that is true."

Linda, beside him, wants to speak, he can feel her opening her mouth and about to say something, but he nudges her. The fewer words spoken the better, he thinks. Then we can all get out of here. He thinks, all she wanted from us really was love, but we couldn't give it; how can you give someone love who's never had it for so long, her need is like a great gaping hole, ready to swallow you up?

The judge is asking Linda,"Did you know that your husband had a key to the apartment in which Plaintiff was living?"

"No. I mean, yes. I know he had one. I know he didn't use it to go into the apartment."

"Except to fix the plumbing, that one time," says Abe. He begins to feel things moving and shifting around him. Nothing is stable, not even the floor. The air conditioning makes it hard to breathe. But the judge is yawning. Perhaps this is a good sign. Perhaps the judge wants his lunch and a nap, perhaps he can't bear to hear one more word of this garbage either. Perhaps the judge is about to freak out.

Plaintiff, who is the woman called Lacey, who looks neither young nor frail nor in need of support this morning, leans forward and points a bony finger. She is shaking, Abe sees, trembling like a horse at the end of its race. She opens her mouth.

The judge waves the air as if she were a fly, not a horse at all, and she has to sit down, with things unsaid.

"So," he turns to Abe, "You did use that key to get into her apartment."

"Just once. With her permission. To fix the plumbing. The toilet was leaking."

"Ah." The judge, who is slim and Hispanic, consults his notes. "The toilet, listed here among the things in the apartment which did not work. You fixed her toilet."

"Yes, I did."

"And you went in there with this key for no other purpose?"

"No, your honor, I did not."

The judge is still for a moment. A moment passes in which he neither moves nor speaks. Everyone else in the courtroom is still too. Abe is aware of Linda at his side, her hardly perceptible shift, an inch away from him. She too is weighing him in the balance. She isn't sure. He isn't sure himself. Suddenly, he can't remember.

Then Lacey stands up and begins to scream out her anger, the long withheld stream of it.

"He did! He did! He came in and he, you won't believe me, you'll not fucking believe me, nobody believes me, I've got notes, your honor, times and dates, I'll tell you everything, he —"

The judge looks at her, then at Abe. He looks at Abe for a long time, as if he knows him, or has heard this before. Abe looks back. If ever there is a case for brotherhood, for male bonding, for a guy simply being on your side because it's the side of reason, not madness, Abe thinks, it's now. He sees the brown eyes upon him. The judge speaks, sounding tired.

"Case dismissed," he says.

The young man who came early on a Saturday morning was large and solid and cheerful, and he wasn't an exorcist but a bailiff. Lacey's mountains of belongings, her trunks and boxes, her cases and files, her computer, her stacks of clothes were all out on the sidewalk. The same unknown man who brought them up the stairs those months ago, carried them down. Lacey herself sat up there in the attic room huddled, holding the tomcat, who yowled and tried to escape. She would not leave, she said. She knew her rights. She would stay there, suffering, to the last possible moment.

When she left at last, hustled down the steps by the bailiff, she hid her face like a criminal leaving a courthouse; or like a woman with injuries too hideous to be seen. All they saw was a glimpse of the wrapped figure, shrinking from view.

So This Is How The World Ends

ALYSON MATLEY

There were nights when, in a deep still sleep, Rachel dreamed of an explosion so world-ripping that her eyes flew open to the volatile silence of the night. For breathless moments she would lie still and search her growing awareness to find the source. Although the explosion gave her the sense that everything she knew was blown apart, she was strangely peaceful. Slowly the familiar room took shape around her. The muffled snores of Donald sleeping beside her would fill the silence. The quiet darkness coating her eyes finally told her that the shattering blast had been within her. Coming full awake she would know that she had dreamed of her own death.

Or so she believed until today. Now, sitting behind the wheel of Donald's car, watching one of the hitchhikers climb into the back seat, she would have welcomed the silent explosion of the night. At least then she wasn't afraid.

"We really appreciate the ride," he said as he closed the rear door. A thick, vaguely sweet odor seeped from his unwashed body and filled the car. Rachel looked sideways at the woman who had climbed into the front seat beside her. There were great scab-covered sores at the corners of her mouth. The woman's body was bloated and braless.

They were the first hitchhikers Rachel had ever picked up. Even back home in Vermont, where life was mostly quiet and people were never thought of as dangerous — even there Rachel drove past hitchhikers, her eyes set in an uneasy stare at the road ahead. Donald would tease her, "Don't tell me you feel guilty because you have a car and they don't!"

But it wasn't guilt, exactly, that kept her from looking at them. She was afraid of their need, as if acknowledging them somehow made her vulnerable to some unknown threat.

Now she was sitting behind the wheel of Donald's Audi with two passengers that seemed to Rachel barely human. And she felt that, like animals, they could sense the terror shooting electric currents beneath her skin.

"Where are you headed?" The normalcy of her voice surprised her.

"Stock Island, we gotta get my dog outa jail." The man had the ageless look of the street-weary.

Thirty miles. Wordlessly, Rachel pulled out and headed south on US 1. Adrenaline pumped a hot fever through her body.

Here in the Florida Keys she had learned that there were indeed people that could be called dangerous. Crack and crime and other more vague pestilence festered in this hot, sticky climate. In Vermont there was an order to life, a feeling that the cold kept things sterile and controlled. But Donald had been transferred and she had been forced to leave the solid sanity of New England. She could make no sense of these steamy, white, dust-encrusted islands where unimaginable debauchery was cloaked in the sweet scent of jasmine. Now all of the uneasy fears that this new world stirred in her took shape in these dirty bodies she had somehow invited into the car.

It was odd, really, but when she woke to those soundless explosions in the night — her dreams of oblivion — she never reached for Donald, never sought the reassuring comfort of his warm sleeping form under her shaking hand. Now, as this irrational fear sparked and coursed through her, her mind didn't reach out for him. An intense clarity and isolation sent her mind reaching only to the car around her. Her mind caressed its new tires, took comfort in the power centered under her foot.

"So, did you run out of gas?" Her voice sounded loud and false in her ears. The man in the back laughed and Rachel could see gaps where teeth belonged.

"Gas? We don't have a car, man!"

Rachel's head swam. Gas had been the reason Rachel had stopped. From a distance, moving quickly, she didn't notice that they were toothless and dirty. She only saw what appeared to be a red gas can and the man's palms pressed together in a silent plea. Those praying hands, a haloed image of need and salvation, accompanied by the stuffy smell of wet wool and wood smoke, murmured amens and mysterious black bibles worn thin by strange hands. The frightening magic of a small stone church came barreling from the recesses of her childhood, stopping the car.

A couple, out of gas thirty mangrove-filled miles from Key West, praying for a charitable driver. She knew it would be a long time forgetting his pleading hands if she were to pass them by.

And so she had stopped.

Her false voice laughed. "I thought you were carrying a gas can — that red thing."

"This is just my stuff," he said. "I'm Tinman and this is Susie."

"I thought your pack was a gas can." It sounded as if she were lying. "I usually don't pick up hitchhikers."

"Well, thanks. One more night and those assholes at the pound might have killed Dog."

Tinman leaned back, settling himself as if he had just noticed how luxurious the Audi's back seat was.

"She's been in there a couple weeks already," he said. "They threw my dog in jail when they threw me in jail." Both he and Susie burst out laughing. Rachel's hands gripped the steering wheel tighter.

"So where do you live?" Susie asked. Her voice was raspy and her breath foul.

It was ludicrous. Here she was, Rachel Driggs who grew up on Long Island and actually had a coming out party, making small talk with two dirty street people who were lodged like a nightmare in the backseat of her husband's expensive car. Small talk when her fear was so real it was nearly choking her. She thought again of the red pack. What could it hold? Alcohol? Drugs? Maybe a gun or a knife.

"We live on a boat." Susie's voice was aggressive.

Rachel goosed the gas up a notch. The smooth, quiet motor of the Audi seemed to hesitate — it felt like a small hiccup — then sped up.

"Feels like the fuel injectors need work. If you wanna wait, I'll have a look at 'em after I get Dog out of jail." Tinman stared at the back of Rachel's head.

Rachel almost laughed at the image: this tall, lanky derelict bent under the hood of Donald's Audi. She smiled in the mirror, but didn't answer.

"Yeah, I guess you're right. I don't look like somebody to be messing around with a fancy German car like yours." Tinman paused and sucked at his remaining teeth. "I'd surprise you, though; I used to be a hell of a mechanic. Specialized on foreign imports. Don't take much to foul the injectors on these cars. Better have it looked at."

"I'll do that." Out of the corner of her eye Rachel saw Susie move and realized that her purse was on the console between them. Frantically her mind catalogued its contents: a wallet with two credit cards, a hairbrush, a new pack of sugarless gum, and a checkbook folded around seven hundred dollars in cash.

Donald had handed her the cash that morning as she dropped him at the airport. "Damn, honey," he'd said, "I forgot to put this in the bank. Could you work a trip to the bank into your busy schedule? Thanks, hon." Then he kissed her on the forehead and ran. She hated it when he sounded like a made-for-TV movie, calling her 'hon,' condescending and smug. She had shoved the money in her purse, glad he would be gone for four days, vaguely contemplating the things she wished she could do while he was away.

"Want some gum?" she asked her passengers as she reached for her purse. When they both declined, she rummaged a piece out for herself, then wedged her purse between her left leg and the car door.

"Hey, Tinman," Susie's harsh voice rasped, "I think she's afraid I'll swipe her purse."

Rachel's head swam with terror and a weird kind of embarrassment.

"You think my Susie's a thief?" Tinman seemed to swell until he filled the back seat. Rachel tried to answer but only a small grunt came out. Tinman leaned forward and put his face up next to her ear.

"Pull the car over. Stop the fucking car!" It sounded like a growl so close to her face. Her rigid arms swerved the car into the path of an oncoming convertible. Rachel let out a small cry as she corrected the wheel and took her foot off the gas. The Audi jumped off the pavement onto the white shoulder. She slammed on the brakes, sending a rooster tail of white coral dust up in the car's wake. It skidded further off to the right and into a stand of mangrove.

Rachel couldn't open her eyes. She was afraid she'd see his huge angry face filling the rearview mirror. She knew that look, that irrational hatred. She knew that the blows would follow. Every time she failed, Donald looked at her that way. And then he hit her. But Donald always apologized. This was a stranger, a derelict with a beer and maybe a gun in his gas-can-red pack. She knew that if he hurt her he'd never come back and make things okay, the way that Donald did.

Rachel leaned her head against the wheel and tried to catch her breath. Susie stared at her, muttering.

Tinman opened the back door and slowly gathered up his pack. "Jesus, lady, you coulda killed us."

Tinman climbed out of the car. "Come on Susie. We'll be lucky to get a ride before the pound closes." He spit on the ground and leaned in toward Rachel. "Lady, you picked us up. My Susie ain't no thief."

Susie clambered out of the car and joined him. Together they walked up the road about fifty yards.

Rachel kept her eyes closed tightly. There was no blow, no internal explosion, only the sound of a lone car approaching. She raised her head and peered through tears and the windshield. She watched as Tinman put his hands together, a prayer for the passing motorist.

CHECKMATES

KIRBY CONGDON

Russell adjusted the umbrella to make more shade over the chessboard. "You mustn't stay out here in the sun too long," he said.
"I will if I want to," Alden answered "I got your pawn."

He took a piece off the board.

"Well, I know that," Russell answered. He adjusted the umbrella to make more shade. "And that was a good move. But even so, you still shouldn't get too much sun."

Alden gave the umbrella a shove. "Say it one more time."

"Say what? Check? Not yet."

"Never mind."

"Of course I mind whatever concerns us, like your health."

"I'm sick?!"

Russell looked into the mid-air as if to weigh definitions, and then let his gaze fall down toward Alden. "No, you're too much alive to be sick."

"You just mean that I'm too, well, let's say, opinionated."

"Maybe you are. Maybe not. We've all got a right to our opinions of each other in this world."

"That's why I always vote—and against the opposition."

"Against? Why not vote 'for'? It doesn't hurt to be positive."

"That can be a presumption, what I call living a lie."

"On such a beautiful day?!" Russell parried. "I admit, it does seem like a lie. This weather is unreal, isn't it?"

"I wouldn't believe it was true if I weren't here experiencing it."

Alden absorbed this without any recognition.

Russell went on to fill the silence. "It's strange—not having to shovel snow at this time of year. Where we come from, they're digging out, slipping and sliding, bundled up against the sleet and the wind."

"That's not my fault."

"I know it isn't. I'm just saying," Russell let his palm indicate the earth, "that here we've escaped all that. It's as though the seasons forgot to turn. My point is—and you have to agree—it's a perfect day."

"Perfection is static. But, anyway, it'll pass."

"My, you're in a bad mood this morning."

"Well, it's true isn't it? What good is it to bury one's self in platitudes?"

"Is it a platitude to enjoy reality, to recognize the eternity of the sun?"

Alden ignored the question, and reflected. "You know, what we call 'real' is just that: whatever passes. In fact, there's no time without motion. The real is what's moving in time. Monuments, eternal things, they aren't alive. We can't seek their kind of reality because it's a dead one."

"I remember, now," Alden continued. "I wrote an essay on that notion and got an A for the whole course I was taking in philosophy because of those ideas."

Russell looked at Alden uncomprehendingly. "What ideas?"

Alden continued thinking out loud. "Yeah. I said that without motion there is no time."

Russell was bored. "Great!" he said agreeably.

"Yes, it is. I said that we measure time only by movement." He pointed at his wristwatch. "And that's not the clock's movement; it's the movement of your sun." He gestured upward and stared at Russell. "If the sun were to stop—along with everything else, of course, like the planets, our birthdays, any change—there would be no measurements—and, so, no time."

Russell extracted himself from the instruction. "Well, everything has a beginning and an end. What's done is done. But that reminds me—the coffee. It mustn't get too strong." He got up to go to the kitchen.

Alden nodded. "Exactly. No fuel from the sun, no boiling water, no coffee, no time. And you couldn't start over! You couldn't begin again. It would be over and done with. Thrown out!"

Russell defended himself. "My coffee? I'm not that bad a cook!"

"I was joking," Alden explained.

"I wasn't," Russell retorted.

"Okay," Alden said. "We'll change the subject. How did you sleep last night? I heard you get up."

Russell nodded in agreement, and asked, "Did you simply throw your quilt on the floor last night before I came in to check on you?"

"It was hot."

"You could have called me. Or rung your bell. I would have come in."

"That's why I didn't."

"But I want to be helpful."

"I don't want help."

"Now, you mustn't be like that."

"Like what?"

"You know. I don't have to say it. You're not just stubborn; you're snotty."

"I try my best."

"You succeed."

"I don't take orders."

"I wasn't giving orders. I'm just saying, I'm here and that's for your own good."

"You're here because you're stuck with me when the whole world's out there at your finger tips."

"Oh, now, that's denigrating yourself. And me too! Thank the Lord that you're alive, alert, conscious, among the living!"

Alden replied, "Not everyone is, of course. I agree with you there—when there's been the massacre."

"Oh, you're into that again!"

"I wasn't talking to you. I was thinking out loud."

"Did anyone—besides me—ever say to you that it's rude to be rude?"

"How can I be rude if I wasn't talking to you?"

"Just your not talking is rude."

"Well, then, listen!"

"But I've heard it all before. You're alone and abandoned and unappreciated because of the massacre; all your generation, your friends, teachers, neighbors—I know the litany—have all been killed. But, as I keep telling you, Alden, they just died off, that's all."

"And you say that none of that has happened?"

"Not in the way you put it," Russell insisted.

"Any catastrophe can be seen through rose-colored glasses! Frankly, I'm thinking of me too, not just what can't be helped. I still feel like a lone survivor."

"But you're not alone," Russell interjected. "Everything I do is for you. And for that matter, I could start life over somewhere else if I wanted to. Times aren't that bad," he teased.

Alden said nothing.

"Okay?" Russell queried.

Silence held both of them in suspension until Alden filled it with, "Okay."

Russell changed the subject. "I'm not into the metaphysics of life and death. I'm into getting your lunch."

When the plate was put in front of him, Alden said, "Looks good," as he stirred the coffee cup that was in front of him.

Russell stood over Alden and the plate for a moment, and said quietly, "Thank you."

A rooster crowed in a neighbor's yard. Alden smiled. "He agrees with me. It looks good."

"Those chickens crow all day long," Russell explained.

"Yeah," Alden said. "A recording would be more stable."

"A synthetic rooster? Something you wind up?" Russell asked.

"But you could turn it on and off. Does everything have to be 'au natural' and continually changing?" Alden argued.

Russell replied, "Being natural is being born, being who we are, being *au courant*, to use your French. That's what that rooster was crowing about. He's natural. He's real. He's alive!"

"That's for mere animals, not human beings. All the cats and those chickens we just heard over there don't know what their fate is. We do. We're not natural. Stop-gaps, protocol, positions, boredom, advertisements, television, futility!"

"You've got some replacements?" Russell queried.

"Is civilization, is politics, manners, courtesy, natural?"

Russell replied without hesitation, "If there's any affection for any of that out there, by somebody, somewhere, then my answer is yes."

Alden thought a moment. "Well, keeping it just to affection, you may be right."

"I know I am," Russell declared.

Alden went on. "The trouble is that love and affection are promoted like some product put out by Dupont. But, still, it's necessary to have that kind of sanity, isn't it? But I lost mine."

"Your love or your sanity?" Russell countered.

Alden looked askance.

"Don't worry," Russell continued speaking. "I know you. You're sane. You don't like to admit it, but you know what love is, giving it, or getting it—and taking it."

Alden pulled his head back in fake surprise.

"I do?" he asked rhetorically.

Russell looked back at Alden expectantly. There was no argument.

Both men nodded their heads slightly. Russell turned back to the chessboard and gave his attention to a piece he moved with care and looked at Alden. "Look! I think I've got your king! It's checkmate!" he asserted.

"The game's over!" Alden said, and turned to his coffee.

The Best Possible Outcome

CONSTANCE GILBERT

It was bound to happen eventually: the unflappable Patty Busch was going to end up in trouble. But it took Bet Carey's sudden defection to do it — that and Patty's asthma.

It was the aftermath of a nice summer seafood barbecue hosted by William Vanderhoff and Seth Siegel by their new pool, the cement barely dry. The pool, a graceful shimmering turquoise curve, hugged a landscaped coral rock and foliage backdrop and filled the rear third of their long, narrow yard on Margaret Street. No one was swimming. It was cool for a Key West August night, only about 80, and Patty sat at the shallow end, toward the side fence, her feet soaking on the first step. She gazed unseeing into the vivid water, cradled a nearly-empty longneck of local lager, and heard the laughter-punctuated party talk and faint sound of George Gershwin tunes only as backdrop to her own desolate thoughts.

She looked up and smiled faintly when Pete Williams, her best friend's husband, appeared and gave her a gentle poke in the ribs.

"How you doing, Bucko?"

"I'll live."

"We know you'll live. Need a refill?"

She held the brown bottle up to the light, assessing her supply of Sunset Ale. "Sure. Thanks." Pete trotted off to fetch another brew. Patty tried to take a deep breath and couldn't. Damn asthma, she thought. Something was triggering it, the fragrances or the ordinary summer humidity or just terminal uptightness. Would Bet show up? With MaryLee? She took the prescribed two tokes of her steroid aerosol spray and breathed easier.

"Here." Pete handed her a dripping cold one, patted her on the head and sauntered back to the crowd.

The booze was plentiful, and the usual suspects were there, anyone who hadn't gone Up North for the summer or grabbed a quick vacation. For August, the turnout was gratifying: four dozen typically colorful Key West characters, scattered representatives of the Lambda Democrats and the Literacy Volunteers, the Conch Republic and the arty gallery crowd of painters and theater types, writers and poets. The pros and the wannabees commingled companionably in the cooling, tropical evening. They milled around on the smooth, new deck with its tattoo of shiny nails. It entirely filled the space from the house to the tall back fence, circling the pool. Huge new pots of mature palms and *Philodendron monstera*, assorted succulents and ficus and passion flower were placed attractively here and there. The crowd jostled them for room and lost. It was, however, a lovely space, and it increased the value of the couple's home substantially.

One of the most distinctive things about Key West, though, was that nobody really cared how much money anyone else had or where it came from. They wanted to know about it, but after that it was irrelevant. The same went for academic credentials. One year the Conch Republic anniversary slogan was "The Last Bastion of the Overqualified," and it was the God's truth. Patty's best friend, Elaine Williams, just happened to have a doctorate with honors from Adelphi. It was four years before Patty found out.

So the party, that second weekend in August, was a companionable mix of locals, all friends or friendly acquaintances, a roster of all possible sexual orientations and marital permutations and social, professional, educational and economic levels.

Patty, who had in a flaming instance of prescience been christened Patience, was another local character, quieter than most. Daughter of Missouri snowbirds who discovered Key West in the '40s, she spent entire winters in town from her season in utero until she went east to college. She attended Key West schools each year from November through April, receiving her secondary diploma by virtue of legacy status and 1320 SATs from an excellent private girls' school outside St. Louis, circa 1967. Then, her junior year at Radcliffe, when her dad, a banker, and her mother, a bipolar socialite, set about to close up the unpretentious eyebrow house on the big corner lot on White Street after spring break, Patty declined to relinquish residence. Her parents eventually threw up their hands and let her stay.

Before long she took up with a shrimper, Haley Flournoy, captain of the old Peppy Girl out of the Bight in those days before it became Disneyland, and being tall and boyish and strong talked him into letting her work crew. When they broke up, after she met Bet Carey at the old Monster bar, she drifted a little, waiting tables and such, then landed a job at the library on Fleming Street. In time she moved up through the ranks to the assistant director's spot, the best they could do for her without a degree. But nobody knew more about libraries, or computers, and her employment was secure.

When the elder Busches died, Patty's two shadowy siblings did not contest her sole inheritance of the house. She promptly sold half of it to Bet for one dollar, joint tenancy with rights of survivorship, but otherwise nothing changed. She continued to go to work every weekday and alternate Saturdays, continued to find most of her clothes in the rummage shops and to vacation modestly. Every few years the rumor zipped along the Coconut Telegraph that she was related to the Budweiser Busches, but she only laughed, pointing to her merry map-of-Ireland face, graying raven's wing hair, and green eyes as proof that Germanic heritage was minimal.

She laughed a lot, matter of fact. Maybe part of it was that she drank. Almost everybody in Key West drank, or used to. But it was a good thing Patty did and a good thing she could hold her liquor better than almost anybody in town, because Bet Carey was a drunk. It wasn't a secret; Bet would tell you herself. Some said she'd designed that T-shirt, the one in the Duval Street shops that said "I'm not an alcoholic, I'm a drunk. Alcoholics go to meetings." It was Patty who went to the meetings, the Thursday night AlAnon, every couple of months.

Bet was born and raised in Key West, like her daddy and his daddy before him, all graduates of Key West High. Bernie Carey was a retired sheriff's deputy and knew everybody. He raised his only child alone after her mama ran off with that sailor from Milledgeville, Georgia, and was secure in his faith that if Patty, who had five inches and forty pounds on his little girl, couldn't get her home safe there were scores of law enforcement officers who could and would, no muss, no fuss. Similarly, her job as an administrative assistant with Mosquito Control was protected, although to give her credit she considered it a point of honor to put in a day's work for a day's pay and rarely took a drink before the sun headed toward happy hour.

On the Fourth of July, walking home from the hospice benefit picnic at Casa Marina after the fireworks off the end of the White Street Pier, Bet, staggering only slightly, announced that she was moving to the new condos out on Stock Island with MaryLee Monsey. MaryLee was a co-worker, a childless 30-something Navy wife whose husband spent a lot of time at sea.

It was two months after Bet's 50th birthday, although she was still small and cute and blonde, and no one ever took her for much over 40. Patty had already started thinking of something special for a silver anniversary celebration, even though it was a couple of years away.

The orangey streetlights cast an almost eerie glow over the picnickers trudging home through the pyrotechnic residue of haze and acrid smells.

"You're kidding," Patty said finally.

"No, I'm not. I wish I was. I'm serious. I'm in love with MaryLee." They walked on. "I've been wanting to tell you for two months. Jeez, Patty, I don't want to hurt you. You're my friend. I love you. But we haven't had much spark left for years, and I'm not getting any younger. I gotta go for this. It's my last chance. I just know it."

Patty was silent. She thought she should feel something, pain or shock or something, but she didn't. She was numb. Passing Laird Street, she finally spoke.

"OK," she said.

Bet moved to the guest room that night, began packing the next day, cleared out by the weekend into the Monseys' non-com quarters at Trumbo till the condo was ready. She'd take some furniture eventually, she said. That she owned half the house wasn't mentioned. Then no one in the crowd, not happy hour revelers at Finnegan's or folks at AIDS Help or MCC or frequent flyers at Winn-Dixie had seen her since. Bernie came over the next Saturday, sympathetic but bewildered, torn between his only child and the woman who had become a combination of daughter and son and pal. Awkwardly, he tried to comfort her; on his shoulder, for the only time since Bet's announcement, Patty bawled.

Seth and William, not taking sides, invited both women to the party, but Bet hadn't arrived by nightfall, with or without MaryLee. Patty retreated to poolside and tried not to dwell on the light-filled French doors, the guests' passage to the deck. What will I do, seeing them together? What will I say? Patty thought. She knew she wouldn't lose her composure, but her reputation for constant calm seemed ironic and a little cruel. She chuckled a little, aloud.

"What's funny?" It was Pete again.

"Nothing. Just the irony. The contrast between appearance and reality."

Pete was the only English lit professor at the community college. He nodded. "Refill?" he asked. The night's mantra.

She held her bottle up to the light again, was surprised to find it empty.
"Sure. But Pete, honey, it isn't my legs been broken here."

He shrugged and went off before she could say thanks. Her shoulders tensed at just seeing folks framed by the door. She tried to loosen up, tried to take a deep, relaxing breath and couldn't. Still the asthma. She pulled out the steroid aerosol spray again, sooner than she should have needed it. It loosened up her chest, but she still didn't feel right.

"Here." Pete handed her another longneck. "Scoot over." He sat beside her, dangling his feet, rubber shower shoes and all, in the pool. "Elaine's arguing 18-mile stretch with Bobby."

"Oh, Lord. That dead horse." Patty tried to laugh, coughed instead. Elaine was passionate about vehicle safety on U.S. 1, the narrow umbilicus that connected the Keys with the mainland. She had no use for the folks who preferred Key Deer to people, while Bobby Brodski, who captained one of the local dive boats, adored the deer and had little use for most people. He and Elaine enjoyed their continuing argument immensely.

"You OK?" Pete peered at Patty in the light of the tiki torches. "You're wheezing."

"Yeah. Usual summer stuff," she said. A chill hit her and was gone. Asthma was relentless, but it always gave her five or ten minutes warning. She'd ended up in the ER one night each summer since the disease suddenly appeared. Three summer nights Bet drove, fast, flashing the headlights of the old Toyota, her knuckles white on the steering wheel. If Patty tried to talk, Bet cried, "Shut up! Just breathe!" Would it be tonight? She used the inhaler again, then again. "Pete?"

"Yeah?"

"You bring the car?"

"Yeah. Want a ride home?"

"Probably" — she paused, breathed.

"No problem."

"Thanks." She took a swig of ale, was shocked to find it coming out of her nose.

"Holy" — a gasp — "shit!"

"Bucko, I don't like the way you look."

"Me, either," she gasped, getting two or three words out at a time, "but till I can afford cosmetic surgery, I'm stuck with it." She tried to smile. Her breathing was labored, audible. Then, suddenly, her eyes widened. "Gotta get ER!"

Pete could barely make out the words. She caught his arm, beseeching, struggling to breathe. He grabbed her, lifted her with some difficulty from the water, braced himself to get her up into his arms. Her tortured breathing made him think of a mortally wounded animal.

"Patty, hold on!" he said. But she couldn't respond. "Elaine! Guys! Help!" It took a moment or two for the situation to sink in, for the party chatter to still. "Call 911," Pete screamed. William, twenty feet away, grabbed the cell on the patio table and dialed.

It was the longest five minutes of most of their lives. Someone — later he couldn't remember who — helped Pete carry Patty through the house and lay her down on the front porch, her head in Elaine's lap. She labored for breath, great, tearing gasps that made her ribcage convulse. Peter wondered what he could loosen, but her shorts and T-shirt offered few options. They knew she never wore a bra. Then, quickly it seemed, the gasps lost intensity until she wasn't breathing at all. Her eyes were open, unseeing, her color ashen. Bobby began CPR, which felt like blowing into a bottle.

Soon the whoo-eee-ooo-eee and flashing lights of a Key West Rescue ambulance swung off Truman and squealed to a stop at the curb. There were two medics, a large young man and an equally large older woman, both in uniform white shirts, navy pants. The woman began work on Patty. The man took Elaine aside, asking for basic information. "Walt, get over here! That can wait. We gotta intubate her." While Walt held her head, his colleague skillfully opened Patty's mouth and threaded a long tube through her trachea into her lungs. "OK, bag her!" The medic began to hand pump oxygen into the tube. His colleague manipulated a blood pressure cuff and then spoke into a two-way radio, transmitting vitals to the ER physician. "Looks like full respiratory arrest," she said. Then she listened. Seconds later she jumped to her feet. "Transport," she ordered. "Get the stretcher."

"Affirmative," Walt said. He thrust the air pump into Elaine's hands. "Here. Keep squeezing." And squeeze she did, tears coursing down her cheeks, until he took the apparatus from her. The rear doors of the rig slammed shut, and they screamed off, with Pete and Elaine and a couple of other cars speeding behind.

Four hours later, almost two o'clock, a nurse wearing a pink cardigan against the refrigerated chill came to get them in the waiting room at the medical center. Only Elaine and Pete were still there; they were ushered over to the treatment bays.

"We were real lucky," she said. "We got her back."

Elaine and Peter looked at each other, horrified.

Patty, however, looked better than they felt. Her clothes had been cut off, and cables and tubes snaked out from under the hospital gown, attached to a variety of surfaces: walls, machines, PVC-type mini-pipes. But there was color in her face, and her eyes were clear.

What looked worst was that long tube, which had been attached to the respirator until the massive doses of drugs took effect and she could breathe on her own. The machine was off, but the tube remained, just in case, the nurse said. It gagged Patty; she pointed to it and shook her head.

"Just take it easy," the nurse said. "It'll come out soon enough. Believe me, it'd be worse if we had to put it back in all of a sudden." Patty glared and gagged. "Don't fight it. You've had a very close call — you were dead, honey. We brought you back, but for the best possible outcome, you've got to cooperate. Otherwise, there could be permanent damage."

Her friends, on either side of the treatment gurney, each took a hand — gently, mindful of the IV tubes and EKG cables. "I called Bernie," Elaine said, "told him to call Bet. Want us to call anyone else?"

Patty looked at her, stricken.

"Well, time's up," the nurse said, but Patty clutched their hands so tightly it took them a few moments to extricate themselves. "We'll be sending her upstairs soon. After a day or so, she'll be good as new," she said cheerfully. "No big deal!"

Elaine looked at the woman, incredulous. Pete, sensing an incipient situation, gave Patty a kiss on the cheek not obscured by the respirator tube and pulled Elaine out of the bay. "We'll see you in the morning," he promised.

"We love you!" called Elaine.

Patty, of course, could say nothing.

They ended up keeping her for four days, days of tests and scans and being tethered to EKG wires and what seemed like endless blood pressure measurements and handfuls of medication. Visitors were only allowed from noon till eight, Key West's most common workshift. By Monday afternoon Patty was near stir crazy. She felt quite well by Sunday, although she had a Texas-sized sore throat. Finally, they turned on her phone, and she called her boss.

There's no question, Clarissa Smith said; she was to take all the sick days she wanted.

"How about none?" Patty asked.

"Watch yourself, child," said Clarissa, ten years Patty's junior and a head shorter, "Do what they say, or Mama gonna whup your butt." It was an ongoing workplace joke. Patty laughed. "Need anything?"

"Don't think so. Maybe a new throat. I'll never be able to sing in the Pride Follies again!"

"Thank heaven for small favors," Clarissa said. There was a pause. "Have you talked to Bet?"

Another pause. "No. I don't have MaryLee's number — not listed. Why bother her at work? What would I say?"

"Maybe that's right," Clarissa said. "You need to focus your energy on healing."

"Elaine called Bernie, but Bet hasn't called."

"Well, honey, you just concentrate on getting well."

"Yeah. Thanks. If you need me, you know where to find me."

"Sure do. Talk with you tomorrow."

Patty pushed the off button and stared at the handset. The numbers glowed florescent yellow when it was turned on. She felt the tears start to well up and quickly blinked them back.

Her recovery proceeded at the expected pace, which to Patty felt like the speed of coral growing. "We'll see," the doctor said Tuesday morning when she looked for a promise that she could go home, or home with Elaine and Pete, the next day.

Then late Tuesday afternoon the phone rang, and she heard the familiar voice.

"Well, holy shit, Patty."

"Hi," Patty said. She could picture Bet sitting in her cubicle at Mosquito Control. What happened to the silver-framed photo, the one of herself and Bernie on his boat, laughing out loud with the spray behind them? she wondered. Was it still on her desk?

"It sounds like you had a really bad one," Bet said.

"Yeah, guess so."

Silence. Bet cleared her throat.

"I'm sorry I haven't come over, but —" The hospital was just down the road from Mosquito Control, after all. "Well, you see — oh, damn!"

Silence.

"That's OK. No problem," Patty lied.

"But you really scared the shit out of me, Pat, honest. How are you?"

"OK. Getting better."

"Daddy's worried. He's up in Ocala till tomorrow, something about the retired sheriffs, but said he'd see you soon as he got back."

"I'll probably still be here. They won't say when I'll get out."

"Well, damn," Bet said. "Sorry to hear it."

"Yeah. Thanks."

Silence.

"Not much you can do," Bet said.

"Hey, Bet, could you call again? Maybe tomorrow?" If I just know I'll hear your voice, maybe I'll think of something to say, Patty thought.

Silence.

She knew the request was a mistake. Bet wouldn't call again, probably wouldn't have called at all if Bernie hadn't made her.

"Pat, you don't understand, and I can't explain. I promised. I promised MaryLee I — well, I just can't say. I'm sorry. Real sorry."

"Sorry?"

Bet didn't answer.

Suddenly, it was as if Patty had never heard that voice before. It was the voice of a total stranger. It was the voice of someone she didn't really know, someone who didn't care about her. Not someone so important.

"Get well soon," the strange voice said softly. "Please."

"I'll try. Thank you for calling."

"Sure," Bet whispered, and hung up.

"Bye," Patty said, matter-of-factly, to the silence. She didn't feel tears. In fact, a funny calm started in her chest and spread. It felt warm, almost good, and she smiled a little.

"Bye," she said.

Chicken Wars

BRUCE WEISS

Bonnie was medium height, always well groomed and although she hardly stood out in the looks department, she more then made up for it in other ways. She was a neighborhood fixture, a true Key West quirk.

She drifted in and out of the shadows of the tropical trees and shrubs that lined our neighborhood streets. A sideways glance here and there, a quick movement of her head as if she had thought of something unusual or important, and a certain carefree lifestyle marked her existence.

Bonnie was a chicken, a simple run of the mill Key West street chicken who was first introduced to us as our neighbor Pedro's pet. The novelty of living next to a pet chicken was both entertaining and interesting. Bonnie blended into the quiet neighborhood rather well, equally on a friendly basis with cats and people. Watching Bonnie eat communally from a dish of food with one of the neighborhood cats was in many ways a microcosm of life in Key West. Peaceful coexistence, a sense of sharing and genuine respect was embodied in that simple common experience.

For all her familiarity and gentleness she was just a chicken. There is really nothing pretty about a chicken. But like so many people that we've met who live on the island, in time her physical characteristics became less and less obvious. She was simply Bonnie, somebody's friend, neighborhood acquaintance.

Occasionally a horn from a passing car would shoo Bonnie from one side of the street to the other. In the evenings her melodious cooing added a soothing voice to the sounds of a tropical paradise. For the most part Bonnie minded her own business, routinely pecking in search of those little morsels that a chicken finds rewarding.

The people who lived in our neighborhood near our first Key West house enriched our lives and to each of us Bonnie was a neighborhood fixture. She was a simple yet unique Key West creature that smoothly blended into the vast backdrop of life on the island. She became part of the unconventional life that was so aptly described by the theory that only in Key West was the abnormal, normal.

Bonnie was one of us, maybe more so in a lot of ways. She was a native Conch, something that none of us were. Often when I wrote to old friends about our new home I included a small paragraph about life with a chicken living next door. "There is a chicken that lives next to us" the letters began. I would describe her attributes, embellishing her life of course. Never once did I let on that it was where Bonnie lived, not who she was that was so unique.

Looking back, Bonnie became an innocent victim of an old story that perhaps is not all that unique. One day a new and distressing sound could be heard far off. I'm not certain when I heard it first but I do remember it getting more pronounced by the hour. It was the unmistakable sound of a rooster moving closer to our neighborhood.

The crowing seemed to herald some type of methodical march, like a torpedo slowly honing in on its target. It was like the distant rumblings of thunder at first, its direction unclear. But as one day passed into the next it became unmistakably obvious that it was moving toward our peaceful neighborhood.

Bonnie was aware of the unfolding situation. But she went about her life with only an occasional twitching of her head at the sound of the crowing, something akin to a mime's sudden and awkward movements. The crowing grew increasingly louder, an obnoxious blip sent out from a radar machine stealthily moving closer.

In the darkness of night the rooster's crowing teased us. Was he coming down Truman or was he circling closer to White Street? Was he moving on the roadway or was he moving through backyards or Bayview Park, taking his own sweet Key West time? One moment he seemed terribly close. In the next he seemed distant. This rooster was obviously enjoying his journey, crowing mightily on his steady advance like the trumpets heralding Caesar's approach to Rome.

We greeted our neighbors with concerns about a rogue rooster who seemed to be measuring our wonderfully quiet little corner of Key West. Others had been through the battles before and described the carnage that could be wrought. To us it was a nerve-racking time as we anxiously awaited the coming storm. At night the crowing played with our sanity. Even when faint and barely perceptible it woke us from a deep sleep. It was locusts, plague, incoming ICBM's and worse.

So called experts on the island told us that the rooster knew where Bonnie was living. Nothing could stop his progress. His crowing was nothing personal against us, they said with smiles, simply his love song. My wife questioned anyone who seemed even remotely knowledgeable about birds. Didn't roosters only crow at dawn, she asked? The rooster had become larger than a gunslinger in our minds; the grim reaper and the creature from the Black Lagoon all in one. If he were half as mighty as his crowing he would be a formidable foe.

His triumphant arrival into our neighborhood was marked by what sounded like a trumpet blast. It made my wife Franchesca and I jump from our bed. He must, I was convinced, be six feet tall and weigh two hundred pounds. I peered through the darkness from our second story bedroom window searching the street for the beast, but he stayed in the shadows. I looked wherever I heard his song. He wasn't making things easy.

We closed the windows and put the fan on high. The fan was a joke. When we bought it we simply intended to use it to block out the background noises of an island that truly never slept. When the salesmen pointed out one floor model that he insisted was the quietest ever made, we shook our heads.

We cranked the fan to high to smother the outdoor din that the rooster had created under our window. All we could hear was the roaring blades akin to the engines of the planes that flew over the island. Yet in an instant we knew we were in trouble. Above the screaming of the fan blades was the penetrating pitch of a rooster. Indignant, he crowed louder. He sounded as if he were in the same room as us.

The night was the longest that we had experienced in our little home, punctuated several times a minute by the rooster's aria. "Are you asleep" became the evening's mantra, met irritably all night long with the one word answer, no.

Above the roar of the fan and the crowing of 'our' rooster we could hear shouts from our neighbor's house. They were unintelligible words that held outrage and anger. None of us slept.

At first light I bounded across our bedroom to look out the window. There was still no sight of the critter. And worse, all was quiet. I wanted to see the object of my wrath, the creature that I had delighted in strangling in my mind a thousand times.

The day felt different, probably due to lack of sleep and angst. How long did roosters stay? Had he passed through, hopefully on his way to more fertile neighborhoods? That question was answered while I still surveyed the neighborhood. Like Gideon and the trumpet, a great blast came from a tree.

I ran downstairs and out the front door and stared at the spot where I had heard the terrible sound. I didn't realize that neighbors Arthur and John were to my right, staring at a different tree. When we made eye contact I put on a sheepish smile. Arthur found nothing amusing about what was happening to our neighborhood.

Our foe was crafty. I swore that he could throw his voice better than the finest ventriloquist could at Mallory Square. He teased us with his sounds. He was obviously a veteran of the Key West chicken wars and he knew rookies, untested soldiers when he saw them. He was there, all right, just biding his time before Bonnie was his and we were all driven madly from our homes.

As evening approached our neighbors greeted each other with a different look. No one was as mad as Arthur. When it grew too dark to see I was reminded of the old description about the War in Vietnam. The Americans controlled the days, but the nights belonged to Charlie.

The rooster began crowing shortly after the first stars appeared. He was damned good. When we thought that we had zeroed in on him his next crow was somewhere else. Was there more than one? The thought panicked us. Lost in all of this was Bonnie, an innocent victim herself. She was not a temptress. It could hardly be her fault we thought and said.

The second night seemed to last forever. The rooster's insidious sounds, the roaring fan, Arthur's profanity and Franchesca's crying combined to made me feel as if I were living in a paradise lost to a Satan. Franchesca walked around like a zombie, mumbling incoherently about her loss of sleep.

When neighbors gathered after work the next day there was a sense of being a part of a vigilante group. We plotted, we schemed, but mostly we consoled each other. We were victims, each of us. We could not handle another night. We all agreed to meet under the street light on the corner at the first crowing. It was us against the rooster.

The first crow that night wasn't a mild love song warbled for innocent Bonnie. Rather, it was a personal affront directed against the group that he had no doubt seen planning his execution. There was no going back. With a new resolve and determination each of us left the comfort of our homes to enter the battle.

Arthur had a slingshot. He claimed that given a clear shot he could at least stun our adversary. John had a coconut in each hand, tossing them with a cavalier attitude as if they were ripe grenades. The rest of us on our first rooster raid gathered sticks. We must have thought that roosters were frightened of sticks.

With Bonnie curiously watching our every move, we treaded lightly, waiting for the rooster to breech. We were armed and ready, convinced that if we had to we would use deadly force to protect the sanctity of our neighborhood, not to mention our sanity.

In the blink of an eye the rooster swooped from a tree to the ground and gathered speed, half-running, half-flying away from us. Someone had obviously tipped him off. The charge of the heavy brigade was on. Arthur let fly with a small rock from his slingshot. He screamed in excitement that he thought he had hit it. Why he thought so no one was sure. The rooster looked like the Olympic decathlon champion on the move. The two coconuts were launched, one airborne and the other more of a bowling shot. Neither came close.

We hung around a bit longer on our street, posturing for those who had watched us from their windows. We convinced ourselves that we had been victorious, that the rooster had been frightened away from our neighborhood for good.

The euphoria didn't last long. The next night the rooster returned and climbed thirty feet into a large tree and proceeded to serenade Bonnie all night. Despite several missiles, the rooster continued to crow. None of us slept again.

Desperate times call for desperate measures. Someone in the neighborhood knew someone who knew the guru of roostering. Word spread quickly that before sunset the next day, a Cuban would come, a hired gunslinger who would make short work of our problem. All day we basked in the belief that a combination of muscle, speed, agility, brains, and good old fashioned Cuban know-how would arrive soon to rescue us from the tyrant that held us captive.

We excitedly waited on the street corner. Just before dark a stranger approached, riding slowly toward us on his ancient bicycle. "The rooster," he said. We nodded in reverence, even as we realized that our knight was at least ninety years old.

"The rooster," he said again. This time we didn't nod. I swear I could hear Arthur crying in the dark. John became our spokesperson. He explained everything including an abject scientific analysis of the creature's habits. When he was done the old man spoke again: "The rooster."

Despair hung heavily in the air. We had expected a B-1 bomber and instead a World War One bi-plane had arrived. Before he could say 'the rooster' again a scream came from one of the houses. The rooster had been spotted and he was on the move. The old man was off like the proverbial shot after the bird. He moved so quickly that we were momentarily blinded to what was taking place.

The rooster veered left and right and the old man was only feet, then inches behind the bird. When the rooster pirouetted and reversed field like O.J. Simpson, the old man surrendered no ground. Turning quickly he resumed his high speed chase, zigging when the bird zigged and zagging when the bird zagged. When he ran past he excitedly motioned us to get into the action. The bird soon had eight pursuers. The screaming was intense as we passed through our neighborhood and ran into the next, virgin territory for the rooster, so to speak.

Once out of our neighborhood we quickly realized that we had another problem. The noise from our shouting stirred residents to their front porches to see what the commotion was. I didn't blame them for calling the police. The rooster was quick and stayed in the shadows, unseen. What those people saw was an old man being chased by seven wild men with sticks.

When the rooster kicked it into overdrive and disappeared, the old man turned right and we turned left. We were smart enough to go straight to our homes to avoid any further troubles. For our efforts we paid dearly. The rooster returned just after midnight and broke the national record for crowing decibels.

The mood wasn't good in the neighborhood. Someone said that roosters lived very long lives and that once they were in a place that they liked, they became permanent fixtures. I wondered how much we could get for our house. There was talk of guns but it was just talk.

It was then that a child appeared who eventually became our true savior. He rode his bike into our midst and listened as we spoke. He inched closer and closer. "You have the problem with the rooster?" he said. I wasn't sure if he was asking a question or just summarizing our dilemma. Once again John took the lead and told our sad story with deference to the child's age. The boy nodded as John spoke.

"I can get rid of your rooster," the boy said. The words were spoken casually as if it were the simplest thing in the world. There was no bravado, no machismo.

"How?" demanded Arthur. All eyes shifted back to the boy.

"By getting rid of that," he said, pointing toward another casual observer, Bonnie. "You get rid of the chicken and the rooster got no reason to stay." I had to admit, as did the others in rapid succession that the idea had merit. We hung on the child's every word.

"Go for it," Arthur barked. But before the boy was allowed to proceed, a voice of reason and common sense came forth. "What about Pedro? It's his chicken. We have no right to give away his pet."

It was the voice of conscience speaking. Luckily, we had none. "Go for it," Arthur said again, this time with the sound of vengeance in his voice.

The child calmly walked up to unsuspecting Bonnie. With sudden swiftness the chicken was swept up and swung gently into the boy's arms. In a deft move the bird was stuffed under the boy's jacket. Mounting his bike, our child gunslinger rode off into the sunset.

We lowered our heads and walked back to our homes and to our loved ones. As to what would happen to Bonnie, none of us knew for sure. I had to admit I had a moment of compassion for Bonnie. It wasn't her fault.

That night the rooster crowed again but his song was different. It lacked the bravado that he had once exhibited. There was a dirge like quality to his song.

The next day neighbors hardly spoke to one another. Guilt, lack of sleep, the fear that perhaps we had sacrificed Bonnie plagued all of us. But something different and wonderful happened soon after, silence. The neighborhood was quiet. In the distance and getting further away the rooster's crowing became barely audible. Without Bonnie, there was no reason for it to stay.

Once again windows were opened and our giant fan silenced. Peace and quiet returned. Pedro never said a word about his missing chicken. None of us talked about the incident outside of our own homes.

A week or so later I saw that boy again. When I asked about Bonnie he rubbed his tummy and smiled.

When I jog by the old neighborhood now I don't know any of the new people. They couldn't know of the great street battle that had taken place beneath their windows only a few years earlier, an effort now mostly forgotten. There are no commemorative plaques to mark the final battle.

I suspect that our chicken war was not terribly different from others being fought across the island. It took, however, the measure of a child to teach us that all our efforts were no match for common sense and a great appetite for chicken.

About The Authors

MARGIT BISZTRAY lives with her husband and two children, all fellow mango hunters and leaf people. She writes about food for *Solares Hill* newspaper and also for magazines you've heard of.

BARB BOWERS writes, paints and lives in awe of the cats and lizards and frogs and orchids that hang out at her Key West compound. Her tribute to them in a memoir, *Cats I've Known*, is almost finished.

ROSALIND BRACKENBURY was born in England and has enjoyed living for nine years in Key West. Her latest novel, *Seas Outside The Reef*, is available from John Daniel, Santa Barbara, CA. A collection of her short stories will be out in 2002.

KIRBY CONGDON, raised in rural Connecticut, studied at Columbia University, worked for encyclopedia houses in New York City, read his own work in Greenwich Village coffee houses, and developed ties to the Beat Generation. Ten collections of his poems, two of prose poems, two reference books and a collection of letters have been published and his work is collected by the Kenneth Spencer Research Library at the University of Kansas.

J.T. EGGERS lives in Key West, Florida. A member of the Key West Authors Coöp, her short fiction has been anthologized in *Once Upon an Island* and *Beyond Paradise*. Her critical essays and poetry have appeared in local and national publications. *Coupling*, her second poetry chapbook, was published by Perky Press in 2000.

THERESA FOLEY is the author of *Cetacea*, an adventure novel set in Key West, and a journalist who specializes in writing about satellites and telecommunications. She has lived in Key West for eight years, and more of her work can be found on her website: www.theresafoley.com.

CONNIE GILBERT, a mom and feminist/civil rights activist, journalist and public relations consultant, also is an award-winning published poet, actress, professor and writer of retold fairy tales for the second grade. Reborn in retirement in Paradise, where she is the *Key West Citizen's* theater critic and a *Celebrate!* freelancer, she is passionate about creating poetry and fiction.

C.J. "CONNIE" GROTH is an award-winning photographer whose haunting, iconic images have earned international artistic acclaim. Her photo illustrations of Key West and Cuba are on display at Guild Hall Gallery, 614 Duval St. in Key West.

DAVID A. KAUFELT has published 17 novels, including the prize-winning *American Tropic*, set against Florida's history. He and his wife, Lynn (author of *Key West Writers & Their Houses*) and son, Jackson, have lived in Key West for the past twenty years.

ALYSON MATLEY is originally from Nevada but has called Key West home for a decade. She and photographer husband Kevin Crean returned from an eight-month working adventure in Nicaragua in 2001. Matley has written for a variety of publications around the country, and this is her second contribution to a Key West Authors' Coöp collection. Her work has been recognized with awards from Rolling Stone Magazine, the Oregon Newspaper Publishers' Association, Writer's Digest, and the state of Florida. In addition, she is the founding editor and publisher of *Cayo*, Key West's only literary magazine.

ALLEN MEECE was born in Somerset, Kentucky, in 1944. He has lived in Key West for a quarter of a century and is the moderator of the Key West Poetry Guild. He is the author of *The Abel Mutiny*, a novel about destroyer sailors in the Viet Nam War.

BOB MAYO has lived in Key West since the early seventies. His fiction has appeared in *Solares Hill*, *Paradise*, and the second edition of KWAC, *Beyond Paradise*. He is currently at work on a new collection of short stories and a novel, all based on his Key West experiences. He and his wife Lucy operate the popular Bobalu's Southern Cafe at mile marker ten on Big Coppitt Key.

ROBIN ORLANDI hitchhiked into Key West in the mid-seventies. A poet and website designer, her work has been included in several Key West anthologies. She holds an MA in English from Rutgers University and is currently chasing a BS degree in Multimedia Technology for the Internet, with a focus on live audio and video webcasting. Visit her at www.e-circuskeywest.com or e-mail info@keywestdigital.com

WILLIAM WILLIAMSON was born February 14, 1961. Conch bred and raised like his family 150 years before him, he grew up on tall tales, real adventures, sordid stories, Hemingway, fishing and drinking. Now living in St. Augustine, he is working on a novel and a book of short stories set in the Keys.

BRUCE WEISS lived for many years in Connecticut where he taught high school history for 23 years. He and his wife retired to Key West in 1996, inspired to write by the beauty of the island and the wonderful authors that live here.

About the Key West Authors' Coöp

Mango Summers is the third collection of Key West short fiction published by the Key West Authors' Coöp, a group founded by six writers in 1995. The first two collections, *Once Upon an Island*, published in 1997, and *Beyond Paradise*, in 1999, remain in print and are available at bookstores in the Florida Keys and at online book companies such as Amazon.com.

In KWAC's seven years, more than two dozen writers have been associated with it and have seen their work, all of which is focused on Key West, published in its collections. KWAC is a loosely organized group that has birthed three books out of a love of the craft of writing, a sense of community and much hard work by a few individuals.

We sincerely hope that you find this collection a satisfying body of literary work, representing the diverse voices and lifestyles that mirror the makeup and oddities of our famous little island at the end of the road. Although the efforts involved in producing a work like this usually cause some of us to swear that this is the last time, the contented reader should be advised that our fourth collection will be out later in the decade, and we hope that we will welcome you back like old friends come to visit our island yet another time.

Visit us online at: www.keywestauthorscoop.com.